ROBIN HOOD.

ROBIN HOOD

AND

HIS MERRY FORESTERS.

BY STEPHEN PERCY,
AUTHOR OF "TALES OF THE KINGS OF ENGLAND."

"Merry it is in the good green-wood,
When the mavis and merle are singing."

LONDON:
TILT AND BOGUE, FLEET STREET.
MDCCCXLI.

CONTENTS.

EARLY SCHOOL DAYS.—The Old Sycamore-Tree.—Robin Hood's Youth.—The Outlaws of Sherwood.—Robin Hood and Little John.—Robin Hood and the Butcher.—The Gay Forester. . . . Page 1

OUR SECOND MEETING.—Allen-a-Dale's Marriage.—The Monks' Prayer.—Robin Hood and the Ranger.—Guy of Gisborne.—Will Stutely's Capture.—The Rescue.—Robin Hood and the Beggar. . . . 29

THE THIRD EVENING.—The Outlaws' Sports.—Robin Hood and the Friar of Fountains' Dale.—The Bishop of Hereford.—A Priestly Quarrel.—A Merry Dance. 63

OUR HALF-HOLIDAY.—The Wood.—St. Bartholomew's Day.—Finsbury Field.—The Queen's Champion.—The Outlaw's Pardon.—The Knight of Wierysdale.—Robin Hood's Generosity.—The Abbot of St. Mary's. 87

OUR FIFTH MEETING.—Reynolde Greenelefe.—The Silver Bugle-Horn.—The Sheriff's Pantry.—A curious coloured Stag.—The Sheriff's Couch.—A Rural Fair.—The Monks of St. Mary's.—The Knight's Gratitude. 112

OUR LAST EVENING.—The Sheriff's Complaint.—The Golden Arrow.—Robin Hood's Smile of Triumph.—A desperate Combat.—Wierysdale Castle.—The Sheriff's Death.—The Outlaw's Allegiance and Pardon.—Robin Hood's Rebellion.—His Death. 135

MARRIAGE OF ALLEN-A-DALE .... frontispiece
THE FORESTERS' WELCOME .. .. p. 14
ROBIN HOOD AND GUY OF GISBORNE 46
ROBIN HOOD AND THE FRIAR . ...,.72
THE BISHOP OF HEREFORD 82
THE KNIGHT OF WIERYSDALS . V | 110
THE GOLDEN ARROW 138
THE OUTLAWS' ALLEGIANCE 150

ROBIN HOOD.

EARLY SCHOOL-DAYS.

TALES of Robin Hood and his merry foresters were the delight of my boyhood.

Many an hour which my school-fellows spent in games of cricket or leap-frog, I passed happily away in the rustic arbour that we had built in the corner of our play-ground, deeply intent upon a volume of old ballads that chance had thrown before me. Sometimes a companion or two, weary of the sport in which they had been engaged, would join me in my retreat, and ask me to read aloud; and seldom would they leave me till the school-bell warned us that it was time to return to our duties.

After the tasks of the day were done we had two hours at our disposal before we were again called to study our lessons for the following morning. In these short intervals it was that, forgetting for awhile Caesar, Cicero, and Virgil, freed from restraint, and exulting in health and spirits, we passed the happiest moments of our early days.

Though many years have since glided away, I can recall these pleasures most vividly. Well do I recollect the youth who shared my bed, and who in school hours sat next me on the first form; and well do I remember, as we sauntered together one bright summer's evening through the shrubbery that encircled our playground, his asking me to tell him some tale of Robin Hood. Willingly I complied. There was an old sycamore tree close by, standing alone upon a little lawn. Its weather-beaten trunk was girt round by a low seat, whence, through an opening in the trees, a wide extent of country presented itself to the view. The shrubbery was upon the side of a steep hill, at whose base lay broad and verdant meadows: through these a navigable river winded peacefully along, bearing upon its surface the white lateen sail of the gay pleasure-

boat, or the more dingy brown canvas of the heavily laden barge, that constantly lent a fresh charm to the delightful landscape. Beyond the meadows was a little village, almost concealed by the venerable trees that surrounded it, while, to the left, the white front of some noble mansion glistened afar off, amid the dark tint of the distant foliage. Many a time had I chosen this favourite bench, and now, with my young friend at my side, I again reclined against the broad old trunk. Scarce had we seated ourselves when another of our school-fellows happened to pass by, and at the intercession of my companion stayed to listen to my promised tale.

I endeavoured to recall the earliest mention of my brave hero in the ballads that told of his exploits, and thus began:—

ROBIN HOOD'S YOUTH.

"More than six hundred years ago, in the reigns of King Henry the Second and Richard Cceur de Lion, there lived in the northern part of England a most famous outlaw, named Robin Hood. The daring exploits and curious adventures of this renowned hero have been celebrated in songs throughout almost every country in Europe; and so great a favourite has he always been in England, that, as the old poet says,

" ' In this our spacious isle I think there is not one But he of Robin Hood hath heard, and Little John; And, to the end of time, the tales shall ne'er he done Of Scarlet, George-a-Green, and Much, the miller's son ; Of Tuck, the merry friar, which many a sermon made In praise of Robin Hood, his outlaws, and their trade.'

" Robin Hood, whose true name appears to have been Robert Fitzooth, was born and bred in the sweet town of Locksley, in merry Nottinghamshire, about the year 1160. He was a very handsome youth, with light auburn hair, and dark bright eyes that glanced and sparkled like stars, and was the most expert archer and bravest wrestler among all the lads of the county, from whom he oft-times bore away the prize in their rural sports. One day as Robin Hood was going to Nottingham upon a visit to his uncle he passed by an ale-house, at the door of which stood several foresters, keepers of the king's parks, drinking ale and wine. Young Robin joined the party, and entered into conversation with them, when he learned that the king

had commanded a shooting match to be held at a town close by in the course of the following week.

'"I will be there,' cried Robin Hood with great glee, ' and will show King Henry a good cloth-yard arrow well shot.'

" ' Ha! ha!' laughed one of the foresters. ' Dost thou think that a stripling like thee may shoot before a king"? I' faith, my young fellow, thou must give place to better men.'

" Robin Hood's brow flushed with anger at this slight, and he half drew his dagger from its sheath, but recollecting himself—' I'll wager thee twenty crowns,' he replied, ' that I will strike a deer at five hundred yards.'

"' Done/ cried the forester. ' I bet thee twenty crowns thou canst not. Our host shall hold the stakes while we go into yonder wood.'

"' Agreed,' said Robin Hood ; ' and if I do not kill the deer thou shalt win the bet.' Each then paid twenty crowns to the host, and the whole party set out merrily to the wood. Young Robin strung his noble bow, and chose one of his best arrows, and in a few minutes a hart bounded across the plain. Although the animal was at a considerable distance farther off than the space agreed upon, Eobin would not lose the chance; he drew his arrow to the head, and let fly with such force that when it struck the deer upon its side the poor creature fell plunging to the earth in a stream of its own blood.

" ' Give me the money,' said Eobin Hood proudly, to the host, c if 'twere a thousand pound, I've won the wager.'

" ' The wager's none of thine,' cried the man with whom he had laid the bet. ' Thou hadst better take up thy bow and begone, or by'r lady I'll make thee rue this day;' and thus saying he bestowed a buffet on the young archer's head, while the other keepers stood by and laughed.

" Robin Hood took up his bow as he was bidden, without saying a word, and smiled as he ran away from them across the plain. When he had got some good distance off, he turned round, and aiming at the treacherous forester, let fly a shaft which struck him upon the breast, pierced his heart, and laid him dead upon the spot. Before his companions had recovered from their surprise, Robin Hood sent arrow after arrow among them, wounding some severely, and stretching others lifeless upon the grass.

" The people of Nottingham hearing of this, came out in great numbers to take the "bold young archer, but he had escaped far away before they arrived; therefore, contenting themselves with taking the bodies of the dead foresters, they buried them ' all in a row,' in the churchyard in Nottingham.

" For a long time afterwards Robin Hood dared not show himself in any town or village, as a reward was offered for his apprehension; but he lived in the forests under the green-wood trees, where he quickly met with several other youths who for various causes had been outlawed like himself.

" In these times immense tracts of land, especially in Nottinghamshire and Yorkshire, were covered with dense woods, which generally abounded in deer and every description of game; and as these were the property of the king, rangers or foresters were appointed for their protection, and the penalty against any one who dared to slay a stag was death.

" Robin Hood and his companions cared very little for these rangers, who indeed stood but a poor chance against them. They shot the king's deer whenever they were in want of food, and cooked it well enough by a fire kindled with branches of the royal trees.

" They likewise were sometimes bold enough to stop his majesty's liege subjects upon the highway, and politely request the loan of a few pounds, which was most frequently granted them without their giving any security for its repayment, the poor traveller being glad to escape with a safe body.

" As the young outlaw thus continued to live in Sherwood forest, his superior skill in archery and his prowess at all manly exercises gained him great fame. Many young men joined him in his retreat, and placed themselves under his leadership, so that he soon found himself captain of at least three-score gallant youths.

" Robin Hood and his followers all dressed themselves in cloth of Lincoln green, and generally wore a scarlet cap upon their heads. Each man was armed with a dagger and a short basket-hilted sword, and carried a long bow in his hand, while a quiver filled with arrows a cloth-yard long hung at his back. The captain, besides wearing a better cloth than his men, always carried with him a bugle horn, whose notes he taught his followers to distinguish at a most incredible distance.

" One day Robin Hood said to his men, ' My brave fellows, here have we been fourteen long days without any kind of sport. Stay ye here awhile among the green leaves, while I go forth in search of some adventure. If I want your assistance three blasts on my bugle horn will tell ye where I am.' And bidding them adieu for the present, he shook hands with them, and with his trusty bow in his hand set out on his expedition. He soon reached the high road, where he thought he should most easily meet with something to do, and marched along boldly for a considerable way. Presently he came to a wide but shallow brook that ran across the road, over which there was but one narrow bridge, that would only permit a single person to cross at a time. Just as Robin Hood set his foot upon the plank at one end a traveller appeared upon the other side, and as neither would return they met in the middle of the bridge. The stranger was a tall handsome young fellow nearly seven feet high, but unarmed, except with a stout oaken staff.

" ' Go back,' cried he to Robin Hood, c or 'twill be the worse for thee.'

" ' Ha! ha!' laughed Robin, ' surely thou jestest, man. Were I to bend this good bow of mine I could send an arrow through thy heart before thou could'st even strike; ' and stepping back a pace or two he drew a shaft from his quiver and fixed it ready to shoot.

" ' Thou talk'st like a coward,' replied the stranger; 4 with a long bow drawn against one who has but an oaken staff.'

" ' I am no coward,' answered Robin Hood, ' and that thou shalt see. Stay on the bridge awhile. I'll be with thee again in the twinkling of an arrow.' And laying aside his bow he ran back along the plank, plunged into a thicket close at hand, and quickly returned bearing a good oak branch.

" 4 Now,' cried he to the traveller, ' now we are equally matched; let's fight out our quarrel on the bridge ; whoever throws the other into the water shall win the day, and so we'll part/

" ' With all my heart,' replied the stranger, ' for go back I will not;' and without a word farther he bestowed such a thwack on the head of Robin Hood that his teeth chattered together.

" ' Thou shalt have as good as thou giv'st,' cried Robin, and laid such a blow on the shoulder of his opponent that every bone in his body rung again. At it they then went in right earnest, and thick and fast rattled the staves upon their heads and backs, appearing like men threshing corn. Getting more enraged at every stroke, they laid about each other with so much fury that their jackets smoked as if they had been on fire; but at last the stranger gave Robin Hood a blow upon the side of his head that made him stagger, and losing his balance the outlaw tumbled into the brook.

" 'Where art thou now, my fine fellow *?' cried the victorious stranger, laughing.

" ' Good faith/ replied Robin Hood, ' I'm hi the water, and floating bravely with the tide. But thou art a bold yeoman I needs must say, and I'll fight no more with thee. Thou hast got the day and there's an end of our battle/ Then wading to the bank he caught hold of a projecting branch of a tree, pulled himself out of the brook, and setting his bugle to his lips blew three such loud and lusty blasts that the* woods and valleys echoed and re-echoed them, till they reached the ears of his merry bowmen. In a few minutes they all appeared dressed in their bright green coats, and ranged themselves round Robin Hood, who was lying on the grass to rest his bruised limbs.

" ' Good master,' cried one of them, named Will Stutely, ' what wantest thou with thy merry men *? Hast thou fallen into the brook $'

"' No matter,' replied their captain ; £ this youth and I have had a famous fight, and he knocked me into the water/

" ' We'll duck him, we'll duck him,' exclaimed the men, running up to the stranger, and seizing him by the arms.

"' Forbear! ' shouted Robin Hood. ' He is a brave young fellow, and must be one of us.' Then, springing to his feet, he advanced towards him. ' No one shall harm thee, friend,' he said; ' these merry men are mine. There are three-score and nine, and if thou wilt join them thou shalt have a coat of Lincoln green like theirs, a dagger, a good

broadsword, and a bow and arrows, with which we will soon teach thee to kill the fat fallow-deer.'

" ' Here's my hand on it,' replied the stranger, striking his palm into that of the bold outlaw; ' I'll serve thee with my whole heart. My name is John Little, but thou'lt find I can do much, and that I'll play my part with the best.'

" c His name must be altered/ said Will Stutely. 4 I'll be his godfather, and we'll have a merry christening in the green-wood.'

"A brace of fat does were presently shot, and a fresh barrel of humming strong ale was broached for the occasion. Robin Hood and his followers then stood in a ring, while Will Stutely, attended by seven of the tallest, dressed themselves in black garments that had once belonged to some unfortunate priests, and prepared to baptize this pretty infant. They carried him into the midst of the ring, and throwing a bucket of water over his face, for fear a little sprinkling might not be enough, Will Stutely in a very solemn tone said, ' This infant has hitherto been called John Little; we do now hereby change his name, which from the

present day to the end of his life shall be called Little John.'

"A loud shout from the men made the forest ring again. When this ceremony was concluded, and when Robin Hood had given his new attendant a coat of Lincoln green, and a curiously carved long-bow, they all sat down on the grass to a merry feast. Music succeeded, and their bold captain, in honour of his new guest, trolled forth the following song : —

" ' You're welcome, my lad, to the forests o' green,
Where the wild deer so merrily bounds; Where the foresters bold their gay revels hold, And their bugle-horn cheerily sounds.

" ' Thou shalt be an archer, as well as the best,
And range in the green-wood with us; "Where we'll not want gold nor silver, behold, While bishops have aught in their purse.

" ' We live here like 'squires, or lords of renown,
Without e'er a foot of free land ; We feast on good cheer, with wine, ale, and beer, And ev'ry thing at our command.

0 ' Then welcome, my lad, to the merry green-wood,
Where the wild deer so joyously bounds; Where the foresters bold their gay revels hold, And their bugle-horn cheerily sounds.'

'THOURT WELCOME _MY LAD TO THE MERRYGREAN -WOOD'.'

" Merrily and gaily did they pass the evening; now dancing round some old monarch of the forest, and now listening to the rude but pleasing ditty of one of their companions. At length the sun went down, and the deep shades of the forest began to draw around them. Robin Hood drew forth his bugle, sounded a few notes, and in a minute or two the whole band were dispersed in groups to their huts and caves.

ROBIN HOOD AND THE BUTCHER.

"Shortly after this merry-making Robin Hood was one morning sitting by the way-side, amusing himself with trimming his bow and arrows, when he espied a jolly butcher hastening to market with a basket of meat before him upon his horse.

"' Good morrow, my fine fellow,' quoth Robin Hood as he passed by. 'What may'st thou have in that basket there ?'

"' What's that to thee,' replied the butcher: ' thou'lt not buy it I'll warrant me.'

"'Nay, now, my good friend, be civil,' returned the outlaw, rising from the grass, and patting the man's horse upon the neck. ' What value settest thou upon this beast of thine, and the basket, altogether ? *

"' Well! an thou mean'st to buy,' answered the .butcher, still doubting, ' thou shalt have the whole lot for four silver marks.'

"' Throw that greasy frock of thine into the bargain,' said Robin, ' and here's thy money: ' at the same time he took some silver pieces from a leathern pouch that hung from his girdle, and held them to the butcher. With great joy at having made so good a bargain, the man instantly dismounted, and giving his horse's reins to his new owner, he quickly stripped off his outer garment. The bold outlaw as quickly encased himself in it, and, mounting the horse, took the basket from the butcher, and galloped off to Nottingham.

"When he reached the town, Robin Hood made his way to the part where the meat was sold ; and having put up his horse at an inn, he uncovered his basket, and began to sell its contents. He knew very little and cared very little about the price that was usually paid for meat, and the ladies in the market quickly discovered that he gave about five times as much for a penny as any other butcher. His stall was soon surrounded, and his brethren in the trade were left without a customer. At first they could not imagine what could be the reason of so strange an occurrence; but when one of them learned that the new butcher had actually sold a whole leg of pork for a shilling, a general council was held, and it was unanimously agreed that he must either be mad, or some prodigal son who had run away with his father's property: but they were all determined to learn something certain about him.

"When the market was over, one of them stepped up to Kobin Hood. ' Come, brother,' said he to him. 'we are all of one trade, come and dine with us to-day.'

"' Eight willingly that will I,' replied the outlaw; ' and a jolly dinner will we have. Tis my first day among ye, and by my faith it shall be a merry one.' They were soon seated at the board, at the head of which presided the sheriff of Nottingham, while ' mine host ' sat at the other end. Robin Hood, being a new comer, said grace, and they commenced a most fearful attack upon divers smoking flanks of beef, and many a goodly haunch of venison. The jovial outlaw did his c duty with the rest, and when at last the dishes were allowed to be taken away, ' Fill us more wine,' he cried, ' let's be merry, my brethren; drink till ye can drink no more; I'll pay the reckoning.'

" ' This is a mad blade,' said the sheriff to his next neighbour; ' we must find out who he is.' — ' Hast thou, friend,' he continued aloud, addressing Robin Hood, 'hast thou any horned beasts to dispose of?'

" ' Aye, good master sheriff, that have I,' answered Robin, ' some two or three hundreds, and a hundred acres of as good free land too as thou'st ever seen.'

" ' I want a few head of cattle,' rejoined the former, ' and if thou wilt, I'll ride this day to look at thine.'

" ' Fill me a bumper of sack,' cried Robin Hood ; 6 here's to a good bargain ;' and tossing off a goblet of wine, he rose up, threw a handful of silver upon the table, and with the sheriff left the astonished butchers to finish their wine and talk of their extraordinary comrade.

" The man of dignity saddled his palfrey, and tying a heavy bag of gold, wherewith to pay for his purchase, to his girdle, set out with Robin Hood to Sherwood forest. Merry were the jokes and loud was the laughter of the bold outlaw as they trotted along the road, and the sheriff thought that he had never met with so pleasant a companion. ' Heaven preserve us,' said he, ' from a man they call Robin Hood, who often frequents these woods.'

" ' Fear not, master sheriff,' replied Robin ; ' ^ saw him in Nottingham town not two hours ago, and Fll warrant me he has not overtaken us.'

" ' In Nottingham!' cried the sheriff, with astonishment : ' why didst not thou tell me that before'? I must go back and capture him.'

"" Twill be a profitless errand for thee,' answered the outlaw. ' Though I know Robin Hood as well as my own self, 'twas with difficulty I recognised him in his disguise.' The sheriff looked hard at his companion, as he claimed so intimate a knowledge with the outlawed forester, but said not a word, only spurring his horse on faster, and keeping as far from his fellow-traveller as the width of the road permitted.

" Presently they arrived at the borders of the forest, and striking into a narrow road that led through it, reached an open lawn of some considerable ex-c 2 tent. Just as they entered upon it, a whole herd of deer tripped gaily across the path.

" ' How likest thou my horned beasts, master sheriff*?' asked Eobin Hood; 'they are fat and in good condition, are they not *?'

" ' I must tell thee, good fellow,' returned the sheriff, reining up his palfrey, ' that I would rather be elsewhere than in thy company.'

" Robin Hood replied by taking his bugle-horn from his side, and blowing three distinct blasts that made the woods re-echo, and his companion's ears to tingle with no small degree of apprehension.

" ' Thou art a knave,' cried he, ' and hast played me false ; take that for payment: ' and the terrified sheriff drew his sword and struck fiercely at the outlaw, who, spurring his steed aside, dexterously avoided the blow. In a moment after, sixty or more foresters, with Little John at their head, burst from the thickets and surrounded the two horsemen.

" ' Welcome, good master;' said Little John to his captain. ; What will'st thou with thy merry men *? '

" ' I have brought the sheriff of Nottingham to dine with ye to-day,' replied Robin Hood; ' make good cheer, and give him of the best/

" ' Aye, marry, that will we/ returned the tall forester, ' for I know he has gold to pay for it:' and gently obliging the sheriff to dismount, he unfastened the bag from the unfortunate man's girdle, and taking his cloak from his shoulders, he spread it upon the grass, and emptied the gold upon it.

" ' Three hundred pounds will serve us for many a carouse,' said Little John, when he had counted the money and replaced it in the bag. ' And now, master sheriff,' he continued, laughing, ' would'st thou like venison for thy dinner *? Hast thou any stomach for a smoking haunch *?'

" ' Let me away,' cried the sheriff, running to his horse's side, ' or you'll all rue this day.'

" Robin Hood sprang to his assistance, held the stirrup while he mounted, and politely wishing him a pleasant journey home, desired to be especially commended to his wife. The poor sheriff, glad to escape sound in body, returned no answer; but striking spurs into his palfrey was soon out of sight. The merry foresters
quickly repaired to their wonted spot, and with many a bumper of ale or wine, drank to the health and prosperity of the liberal sheriff of Nottingham.

ROBIN HOOD AND WILL SCARLET.

" The bold outlaws were afraid to show themselves for some time after this adventure, and for several weeks retired to a distant forest, where their haunts were not so well known as in Sherwood.

" Robin Hood was one morning rambling among the w r oods, when, through the branches of the trees, he caught sight of a gay young fellow walking carelessly along and whistling merrily. The stranger was clothed in a silken doublet of beautiful scarlet, his hose were likewise of the same bright colour, and his gay green cap was ornamented with a crimson feather. By his side hung a handsome broadsword, the hilt of which was studded with precious stones, and in his left hand he carried an elegantly carved bow ; while a quiver of polished oak, inlaid with silver, was suspended by a silken baldric at his back.

"As he emerged from the thicket upon a little plain, on which the noon-day sun was permitted to shine
unobscured by the deep foliage that on all sides surrounded him, the traveller's heart leapt with joy at the sight of a herd of deer grazing quietly at the other end of the verdant glade.

" ' The fattest among ye,' quoth he, loud enough for the outlaw to over-hear him, 'shall serve my dinner to-day :' and drawing an arrow from his quiver, he fixed it upon his bow, and discharged the weapon with such keen velocity that the noblest animal among the herd fell dead at the distance of forty yards.

" ' Well shot! well shot, my friend! ' cried Robin Hood, advancing from his concealment. 'Would'st like to be a forester in this merry green-w'ood ^'

" ' Where springest thou from ? ' said the stranger, turning round sharply at the sound of a voice: ' Go thou thine own way; I'll go mine.'

" ' If thou'lt accept the place,' returned the outlaw, unheeding this angry reply, ' I'll make thee a bold yeoman, and give thee livery of mine.'

" ' Livery!' cried the other. ' By St. George, an thou dost not take to thine heels, I'll give thee such a buffet as shall make thine ears ring for many a mile.'

" Robin Hood drew back a step, and bent his ever-ready bow, and at the same time the stranger, quick as thought, drew another arrow from his quiver, and pointed it at the outlaw.

"' Hold ! hold !' cried the latter. ' This is cowards' play. Take thy sword, man, and let's fight it out under yonder tree.'

" ' With all my heart,' replied the traveller; ' and by my faith I will not leave thee till thou dost cry " 'a mercy." ' Then laying aside their bows, each drew his sword, and stepping beneath the shade of a broad old oak, began the combat in right good earnest. The bold outlaw, seizing an unguarded moment, laid a blow upon the shoulder of his opponent that made him wince again; but, in retaliation, the stranger rushed furiously at Robin Hood, and struck him so violently upon the head that the blood ran trickling down from every hair.

"'Mercy, good fellow—mercy,' he cried, dropping his sword's point to the earth, and leaning himself against the tree; ' thou hast fairly beaten me. Tell me,— who art thou *? and what seek'st thou here 1 '

" ' Ha! thou alterest thy tone now,' answered the victor with a laugh; ' but, if thou'rt a true man, thou may'st stand my friend. Know'st thou where dwells a yeoman they call Eobin Hood ? '

"' Wherefore dost thou seek him ? ' inquired the outlaw.

" ' I am his sister's son,' replied the youth. ' I had the misfortune to slay my father's steward in a quarrel, and am forced to flee from home.'

" ' Thy name *?' asked Robin Hood anxiously.

" ' Is Will Gam well, of the town of Maxwell,' replied the stranger.

" ' My brave boy, I am thine uncle,' exclaimed the outlaw, clasping him in his arms with delight; ' thou should'st have said this before we shed each other's blood.'

"'Forgive me — forgive me,'—cried the youth, bending on his knee; ' and I'll serve thee day and night.'

" ' Give me thy hand,' replied Eobin ; ' thou art a bold fellow, a true marksman, and a right valiant swordsman, as I know to my cost. Let us go seek my merry men.' And with many a pleasant discourse the newly-found relations beguiled their path to the haunt of the outlaws. As they approached the spot, Robin Hood drew his bugle from his girdle, and sounded a few short notes. Before the music had ceased Little John stood at his side.

"' Is danger at hand, good master ?' he said. 'Where hast thou tarried so long? Whence this blood? 5

" ' I met with this youth,' replied Robin Hood, c and full sore has he beaten me.'

" c Then I'll have a bout with him,' cried the tall forester, and see if he will beat me too;' and with a staff in his hand he stepped before the stranger.

"' Nay nay,' said his captain, interfering, ' that must not be; he is my own dear sister's son, and next to thee shall be my chief yeoman.'

"' Welcome, my friend, to merry Sherwood,' exclaimed Little John, shaking the new comer by the hand. ' We'll have a rare feast for thee to-night. But by what name shall we call thee among our jovial comrades ? '

"' His name is Gamwell,' replied Robin Hood; ' but we had better re-christen him as we did thee ; he has forsooth a fine scarlet doublet, and Will Scarlet shall be his name.' Then again taking his bugle, he set it to his lips, and winded it till

"' The warbling echoes wak'd from every dale and hill.'

" More than a hundred tall yeomen, clad in Lincoln green, soon attended this summons, bounding among the trees like so many playful deer.

" Will Scarlet, frightened at the sight of so many men, all armed with bows, cried to his uncle to fly from them, and was himself starting off at his full speed, when Robin Hood caught him by the arm, and laughing heartily at his terror, bade him behold his future companions.

" ' What want'st thou, good master $ ' said Will Stutely, the leader of the band. ' Thy bugle sounded so shrill we thought there had been work for us.'

" ' The danger's over now,' replied Robin Hood; ' but welcome your new comrade; he is my own sister's son, and has proved himself a gallant youth, for he has given me a famous beating.'

" The foresters set up a simultaneous shout, and each advancing in his turn took the hand of the delighted youth. The rest of the day was spent in feasting and sporting, till the departing rays of the sun warned them to their caves and bowers."

Just as I had thus concluded, and my young companions were making their various remarks upon the merry life of the bold outlaws, the deep tone of our school-bell rang in our ears. Off we started, like a herd of deer frightened at the notes of Robin Hood's bugle-horn.

OUR SECOND MEETING.

ROBIN HOOD AND ALLEN-A-DALE.

ON the next evening, when I took my seat beneath the sycamore, I found that it was surrounded by no less than six of my school-fellows ; so popular had been the legends of Robin Hood with my hearers of the previous day. I was mightily pleased at this, and with renewed confidence began the following tale : —

" Shortly after the accession of Will Scarlet to his company, Robin Hood was one morning roaming through the forest, when he beheld a young man, very elegantly dressed in crimson silk, skipping merrily over the green plain, singing a roundelay; his face was lighted up with gladness, and his heart seemed overflowing with joy.

" On the very next morning Robin Hood again encountered the same youth. All his finery was gone. He wore a russet suit, and his countenance was overspread with melancholy. He walked slowly, absorbed in meditation, and now and then broke out into exclamations of the keenest grief. The outlaw's heart was moved. ' What can have caused this sudden change,' he said to himself: ' perhaps I may relieve his sorrows;' and emerging from the grove he stood before the young man's path.

" ' What ailest thou my friend ? ' he said to him; ' but yesterday thou wert as gay as a lark, and to-day as thou wert at a funeral.'

" ' Why dost thou ask ?' said the youth : fi thou canst not help me in my distress.'

" * I have a hundred as good yeomen as ever drew bow in the green-wood,' replied the outlaw, ' that will do my bidding as I list.'

"' Lend me thine aid,' cried the young man eagerly, * and I'll be thy true servant for ever. My name is Allen-a-Dale. But yesterday I was to have wedded the fairest maiden upon whom the sun ever shone. To-day she is taken from me, and will be forced to marry a rich old knight whom she detests.'

" ' Where is the wedding to take place,' inquired Robin Hood.

u ' At the little church in the vale 'twixt here and Nottingham,' replied the lover; ' 'tis not five miles distant.'

" ' We will try what's to be done,' rejoined Robin. ' Come with me, and by my faith it shall go hard but thou gettest thy fair maiden yet; ' and taking the now, hopeful youth by the hand, the outlaw led him away.

" Great preparations were made for the approaching wedding in the village church that Allen-a-Dale had mentioned. The lord bishop of the diocese was there, dressed in his gorgeous robes; and the cottagers, decked out in their holiday costume, were waiting anxiously to witness so grand a marriage. An old man with a long flowing beard likewise demanded and received admission into the interior of the sacred edifice. He wore a sombre-coloured mantle that entirely covered him, and carried, slung by a belt across his shoulders, a harp, which, as he seated himself near the altar, he placed at his feet, ready to strike on the appearance of the bridal party. Presently the grave old knight entered the church, leading the

beautiful damsel by the hand. Young girls, dressed in white, scattered roses in their path as they advanced, and the harper sounded his noble instrument. The poor maiden seemed totally unconscious of all that passed. She walked slowly, with her head bent to the earth; and tears burst from her eyes, and coursed each other down her lovely cheeks : but the old knight was unmoved, and hurried her to the altar. The bishop opened his book and began the ceremony.

"' I forbid this match,' exclaimed a voice that seemed to proceed from where the harper sat.

"The reverend father, surprised at so un%sual an interruption, stopped, and looked around: —'Stand forth, whoever thou art, and state thy reasons/ said he, after a long pause.

"' This old knight is not the damsel's free choice,' cried the old man, rising from his seat. c and I forbid the marriage.' At the same moment pulling away his false beard, and casting aside his cloak, KOBIN HOOD drew a bugle-horn from his baldric, and stunned the ears of bishop, knight, and maiden, with the loudness of his blast. At the summons four and twenty yeomen darted out of a grove that was close at hand, bounded like wild deer over the plain, and quickly entered the church. The first man among them was Allen-a-Dale. He ran to Robin Hood, and gave him his trusty bow; then, rushing to the altar, he hurled the old knight aside, and clasping the lovely maiden in his arms, bore her to the outlaw.

"' Now, my good lord bishop,' said Robin Hood, c thou may'st marry this fair lady to her own true love.'

" c That cannot be,' returned the bishop, closing his book with a loud clap; ' the law requireth that the banns be published three times in the church.'

"' We will soon remedy that,' cried Little John, stepping forward from among the bowmen. ' Lend me thy gown awhile, good master bishop, and I will do that office;' and as he spake, he entered the enclosed space by the altar, and stood by the side of the reverend father, who, with a very ill will, suffered his robe to be taken from his person.

" The foresters and villagers, one and all, could not restrain their mirth when the tall yeoman put the garment upon himself, and took up the bishop's volume. For fear that thrice might not be enough, he pub-lished the banns seven times, while Allen-a-Dale and his betrothed took their places at the altar steps.

"' Who gives away this maid ? ' asked Little John when he had finished that part of his duty.

"' That do I,' answered Robin Hood, who stood at the damsel's side. 'Where's the man who dares dispute my gift ?' and clapping the bridegroom upon his shoulders—' Cheer ye, my gallant friend,' he cried ; ' by my troth thou hast boldly won the fairest maiden in Christendom.'

" Neither the old knight nor the bishop interposed, but while Little John proceeded with the ceremony they both left the church. As soon as all was concluded, the young girls again strewed flowers in the path of the now joyous bride, the bells struck up a merry peal, and the villagers and foresters, rushing out of the church, greeted the happy pair with loud shouts of joy. Robin Hood and his men escorted them home, and having drunk to the welfare and happiness of young Allen-a-Dale and his fair lady, they again returned to their green-wood shades.

ROBIN HOODS GOLDEN PRIZE.

" There were many days in which the outlaws of Sherwood scarcely knew how to pass away their time. They often grew tired of their easy and careless life, and longed for an adventure where more active exertions would be required. Robin Hood, especially, could ill brook the monotony of a forester's life. He was ever bent upon some enterprise, either by himself alone, or with the assistance of his followers ; and rarely a week passed but that the bold captain threw a good store of gold into his treasury. One day he disguised himself in the dress of a friar. A long dark-coloured gown completely covered his green doublet, and a large cowl over his head nearly concealed his features. His waist was girt round with a white woollen rope, from which were suspended a string of beads and an ivory crucifix. Thus attired, with a staff in his hand, he took the high road, and trudged on merrily. The first persons he met were, an honest husbandman, clad in tattered garments, carrying a chubby boy in his arms, and his wife, with an infant, following mournfully in his steps. Robin Hood stopped D 2 them, inquired the cause of their grief, and learned that their cottage had been burned down by a party of marauders, and that they were then on their way to Nottingham, where the poor man hoped to obtain employment.

" The seeming priest, moved with compassion at their forlorn state, drew forth a broad piece of gold and gave it to the wanderers, who ever after blessed the day they met the generous friar.

" Robin Hood walked on nearly a mile farther without meeting a single traveller, when at last he espied two monks in black gowns coming towards him, riding upon mules.

"' Benedicite,' said Robin Hood meekly, as they drew near him ; ' I pray ye, holy brethren, have pity upon a poor wandering friar, who has neither broken bread nor drunk of the cup this day/

" ' We are grieved, good brother,' replied one of the monks, 'we have not so much as a penny. Robbers met us on the way, who have stripped us of all our gold.'

"' I fear thou tellest not the truth,' returned the friar. ' Wherefore did they leave ye those beasts ? '

"' Now by'r lady/ cried the second monk, ' thou art an insolent fellow,' and pushing on their mules he and his companion galloped off. The outlaw laughed at their precipitate decampment, then starting off at his best speed, he soon overtook them. c Brethren,' he cried, as one after the other he pulled them from their saddles, ' since we have no money, let us pray to our dear lady to send us some;' and falling on his knees he made the monks kneel down beside him. The old ballad says

"' The priests did pray, with mournful cheer,
Sometimes their hands did wring,
Sometimes they wept and cried aloud,
Whilst Robin did merrily sing.'

" After some time thus spent, the outlaw rose. ' Now, my brethren,' quoth he, ' let us see what money has been sent us — we will all share alike;' and putting his hand in his pocket he pulled forth twenty pieces of gold, and laid them on the grass. The monks fumbled a long time amid their garments, but could find nothing.

" ' Let me search,' cried the friar; ' perchance ye have not hit upon the right pocket.' The monks

reluctantly consented, and presently the outlaw drew forth two purses, and counted out five hundred golden crowns.

" ' Here is a brave show/ said Robin Hood,

' Such store of gold to see; And ye shall each of ye have a part 'Cause you prayed so heartily.'

" He then gave them back each fifty pieces, which the monks eagerly seized, and running to the side of their mules they were about to ride off. 'Stay/ cried the outlaw ; ' two things ye must swear: first — that ye will never tell lies again; and secondly — that ye will be charitable to the poor.' The priests fell on their knees and gave the required promise to Robin Hood, and then

" ' He set them on their beasts again,

And away then they did ride; And he returned to the merry green-wood With great joy, mirth, and pride.' "

" Can you remember the whole of any ballad ? " asked one of my hearers. "If you could I should like very much to hear it."

" And so should I."— " And I."— "And I."— cried two or three other voices.

" I fear there will be some parts that you will scarcely understand," I replied; " but as you wish it, you shall hear of

ROBIN HOOD AND THE RANGER;

OR, TRDE FRIENDSHIP AFTER A FIERCE FIGHT.

" When Pho&bus had melted the ' sickles' of ice,

And likewise the mountains of snow, Bold Robin Hood he would ramble away, To frolic abroad with his bow.

"He left all his merry men waiting behind, Whilst through the green valleys he pass'd, Where he did behold a forester bold, Who cry'd out, ' Friend, whither so fast ?'

"' 1 am going,' quoth Robin, * to kill a fat 'buck, For me and my merry men all; Besides, ere I go, I'll have a fat doe, Or else it shall cost me a fall. 1

"' You'd best have a care,' said the forester then, 'For these are his majesty's deer; Before you shall shoot, the thing I'll dispute, For I am head forester here.'

40 ROBIN HOOD AND THE RANGER.

"' These thirteen long summers/ quoth Robin, ' I'm sure, My arrows I here have let fly; Where freely I range, methinks it is strange You should have more power than I.

"' This forest/ quoth Robin, * I think is my own, And so are the nimble deer too; Therefore I declare, and solemnly swear, I'll not be affronted by you.'

"The forester he had a long quarter staff, Likewise a broadsword by his side; Without more ado, he presently drew, Declaring the truth should be tried.

"Bold Robin Hood had a sword of the best, Thus, ere he could take any wrong, His courage was flush, he'd venture a brush, And thus they fell to it ding dong.

"The very first blow that the forester gave, He made his broad weapon cry twang; 'Twas over the head, he fell down for dead, O that was a terrible bang!

"But Robin he soon recovered himself, And bravely fell to it again; The very next stroke their weapons they broke, Yet never a man there was slain.

"At quarter staff then they resolved to play, Because they would have the other bout;

And brave Robin Hood right valiantly stood; Unwilling he was to give out.

"Bold Robin he gave him very hard blows,
   The other return'd them as fast; At every stroke their jackets did smoke ; Three hours the combat did last.

"At length in a rage the forester grew,
   And cudgel'd bold Robin so sore That he could not stand, so shaking his hand, He cry'd, ' Let us freely give o'er.

" ' Thou art a brave fellow, I needs must confess
   I never knew any so good; Thou art fitting to be a yeoman for me, And range in the merry green-wood.'

" Robin Hood set his bugle horn to his mouth,
   A blast then he merrily blows; His yeomen did hear, and straight did appear A hundred with trusty long bows.

"Now Little John came at the head of them all,
   Cloth'd in a rich mantle of green; And likewise the rest were gloriously drest, A delicate sight to be seen !

"' Lo! these are my yeomen,' said bold Robin Hood,
   ' And thou shalt be one of the train, A mantle and bow, and quiver also, I give them whom I entertain.'

" The forester willingly entered the list,
   They were such a beautiful sight; Then with a long bow they shot a fat doe, And made a rich supper that night,

"What singing and dancing was in the green-wood,
   For joy of another new mate! With might and delight they spent all the night, And liv'd at a plentiful rate.

" Quoth he, ' My brave yeomen, be true to your trust,
   And then we may range the woods wide.' They all did declare, and solemnly swear, They would conquer, or die by his side."

This ballad was highly approved of; and when, as usual, a few remarks had been made upon the valour of the champions, I resumed my tales, and told of

ROBIN HOOD AND GUY OF GISBORNE.

" How delightful are the woods upon a summer's morn. The bright foliage of the trees now shines in its deepest verdure; the lawns and glades are clothed with luxuriant grass and sweet wild flowers, upon which the dew-drops glisten in the rising sun. The merry birds sitting upon the tender branches pour forth their morning lays; and yon lark, now soaring high towards the blue expanse of heaven, makes hill and dale re-echo with her melodious carol; — all telling of the goodness of their Creator, and praising him for his wondrous works. Thus thought Robin Hood as, on a bright morning in the pleasant month of June, he wandered amid the trees of Barnesdale. He had been awakened earlier than usual from his slumbers by the loud and incessant singing of a golden thrush: he arose, and rambled forth, enjoying the freshness of the morning breeze, and the sweet music that was borne upon it. Many a hart darted across his path, and many a young fawn skipped playfully at his side, and then bounded into the recesses of the forest. At another time the outlaw's keen arrow would have followed them, but now he smiled at their merry gambols, and charmed with the loveliness of the scene, he rested upon his bow, and contemplated with heartfelt pleasure the tranquil beauty of the morn. He continued thus, absorbed in meditation, when suddenly a distant sound broke upon the stillness of the air.

" The outlaw listened for a moment. ' 'Tis the tramp of horses,' he whispered to himself; and stepping to a tree, quick as thought he climbed amid its branches. Thence he could plainly distinguish the glitter of spearheads and bright helmets, and scarce had he secured himself from observation, when several horsemen, followed by a troop of soldiers, passed within a few yards of his hiding-place. In the leader, Robin Hood at once recognised his old friend, the sheriff of Nottingham, who he had no doubt was now come with his men to seek for the traitorous butcher of Sherwood.

"It was not till some time after this little band had gone by that the outlaw ventured to descend the tree; and then, striking into a narrow path, he endeavoured to retrace his steps to the spot where his men were dwelling. On his way he was obliged to cross the high road, where a stranger arrested his steps.

"'Hast thou seen the sheriff of Nottingham in the forest*?' he inquired.

"'Aye, my good fellow, and with a fine band at his tail,' replied Robin Hood. 'Art thou seeking him 2'

"'Not him,' returned the stranger, who was a bold yeoman, dressed in a coat of the untanned skin of some wild beast, and who carried a bow in his hand, and a sword and dagger at his side. 'I seek not the sheriff, but him whom he seeks.'

"'And who may that be"?' said the forester, at the same time forming a pretty shrewd guess.

"'A man they call Robin Hood,' answered the stranger. 'If thou canst show me where he is, this purse shall be thine;' and taking a well-filled leathern bag from his girdle, he rattled the contents together.

u 'Come with me, my friend, and thou shalt soon see Robin Hood,' returned the outlaw. 'But thou hast a brave bow; wilt thou not try thy skill with me in archery 4?' The stranger at once consented. Robin Hood with his dagger cut down the branch of a tree, and fixing it in the earth, suspended upon the top a little garland, which he entwined with the long grass. The archers took their station at the distance of three hundred yards, and the stranger drew the first bow. His arrow flew past the mark far too high. The outlaw next bent his weapon, and shot within an inch or two of the stick. Again the yeoman essayed; and this time his shaft flew straight and passed through the garland; but Robin Hood stepped up boldly, and drawing his arrow to the very head, shot it with such vehemence that it clave the branch into two pieces, and still flew onwards for some yards.

" ' Give me thy hand,' cried the stranger, — ' thou'rt the bravest bowman I've seen for many a day, an thy heart be as true as thy aim, thou art a better man than Robin Hood. What name bearest thou *? '

" ' Nay — first tell me thine,' replied Robin, ' and then by my faith I will answer thee.'

"' They call me Guy of Gisborne,' rejoined the yeoman. ' I'm one of the king's rangers; and am sworn to take that outlawed traitor, Robin Hood.'

"' He's no traitor, sirrah,' returned the forester angrily ; ' and cares as much for thee as for the beast whose skin thou wearest. I am that outlaw whom thou seek'st, — I am Robin Hood:' and in a moment his drawn sword was in his hand.

" c That's for thee then,' cried the yeoman, striking fiercely. 'Five hundred pounds are set upon thine head, and if I get it not I'll lose mine own.'

" Robin Hood intercepted the intended blow, and fought skilfully with his fiery and more athletic antagonist, who poured down an incessant shower of strokes

ROBIN HOOD GUY, OF GISBORNE.

upon him. Once the bold outlaw fell; but recovering himself sufficiently to place a foot upon the earth, he thrust his sword at the ranger, and as he drew back to avoid it, Robin Hood sprung up, and with one sudden back-handed stroke slew poor Guy of Gisborne upon the spot. He immediately stripped off the hide from the dead man, upon whom he put his own green mantle; and then taking his unfortunate opponent's bow and arrows and bugle-horn, he drew him into a thicket, and darted off swiftly to assist his men.

" In the mean while the sheriff of Nottingham and his attendants had pushed their way through the woods to Barnesdale, where they had been informed the outlaw was lying.

" The bold foresters, ever on the alert, heard the unusual sound of the tramp of armed men, and with their bugles gave notice to each other of the danger. Little John had been in pursuit of a fat doe, which he was bringing home upon his shoulders, when the warning sounded upon his ears. Concealing his booty among the underwood, he bounded through the forest to the scene of danger, where he found that Will Stutely and many of his comrades were urging their utmost speed to escape from some of the sheriff's men, and two bold foresters lying dead upon the grass. Little John's wrath was kindled. Forgetful of the imprudence of the action, he drew his bow, and let fly an arrow at the cause of this mischief, but the treacherous weapon brake in his hand, and the shaft flew wide of the sheriff, but striking one of his followers stretched him lifeless upon the turf.

" Left almost defenceless by the loss of his bow, Little John could make but a poor resistance to the crowd of men who instantly surrounded him. By the sheriff's order he was bound hand and foot, and tied to a young oak, receiving at the same time a promise that so soon as more of his comrades were taken he should with them be hanged on the highest tree in Barnesdale. Just then a loud blast from a bugle rang through the wood.

" ' Here comes good Guy of Gisborne,' quoth the sheriff; ' and by his blast I know that he hath slain that bold knave, Eobin Hood. Come hither, good Guy,' he continued as the outlaw appeared, effectually concealed in the yeoman's clothing. ' What reward wilt thou have of me ^ '

" ' I must finish my work first, good master sheriff,' replied the disguised hero. ' I've slain the master, and now I must kill the knave; but 'twere cruel ere he has confessed his sins.'

" ' Thou'rt a pretty fellow truly to turn father-confessor,' replied the sheriff; ' but go, do as thou list, only be quick about it.'

u The outlaw stepped to the side of Little John, — who had easily recognised his beloved master's voice, — and pretended to listen attentively to what the poor captive might be saying, but drawing his dagger, he gently cut the cords that bound his comrade, and gave him the bow and arrow that he had taken from Guy of Gisborne.

" Robin Hood then placed his own bugle to his lips and sounded a peculiarly shrill blast, that rung in the sheriff's ears as a death knell, so well did he remember the sound. The two outlaws were quickly supported by a band of sixty foresters, who had collected together, and all drew their bows at once against the intruders. A dense flight of arrows fell upon them. Those who were not too badly wounded immediately set spurs to their horses, or took to their heels in the most abrupt confusion. One poor forester, Will Stutely, they bore off with them. Robin Hood and his men pursued, and it was not till they had got half way on their road back to Nottingham that the defeated sheriff and his attendants drew rein.

THE CAPTURE OF WILL STUTELY.

" Robin Hood was sorely grieved when he learned that his bold follower had been carried off. Calling his men together, he made them swear that they would rescue their brave comrade, or die in the attempt. Will Scarlet was despatched at once to learn to what place he was taken; and hastening with all speed to Nottingham, he found that the news of the terrible affray, and the sheriff's precipitate flight, had already caused a great sensation among the gossips of the town. From them he easily ascertained that the captive outlaw was imprisoned in the castle, and that he was to be hanged on the following morning at sunrise. Scarlet flew back with this intelligence to Robin Hood, who communicated it to his men, and all again swore to bring Will Stutely safely back to Barnesdale, or fearfully avenge his death.

" Early on the morning after his capture, the unfortunate prisoner, tightly bound and guarded on every side, was led from his cell towards the gallows that had been erected on the plain in front of the castle. He cast his eyes anxiously around, in the hope that succour might be at hand, but he could perceive no signs of the presence of his comrades. Turning to the sheriff, who attended in person at the execution of so notorious an outlaw,

"' Grant me one boon, I pray thee,' cried he; 'never has one of Eobin Hood's men died like a thief; let me not be the first. Give me my good sword in my hand, and do ye all set upon me. I shall then die as a brave man should.'

"' I've sworn to hang thee on the highest gallows in Nottingham,' replied the sheriff; ' and when I catch that still greater villain, Eobin Hood, he shall dance by thy side.'

"' Thou'rt a dastard coward!' cried Stutely in a rage, ' a faint-hearted peasant slave! By'r lady, if e'er thou meet'st bold Robin Hood, thou'lt have payment for the deed thou'rt doing. He scorns and despises thee, and all thy cowardly crew, who will as soon take

E2

King Henry prisoner as brave Robin Hood;' and the forester laughed loudly in defiance.

" At the sheriffs command the executioner seized him by the arms, and hurried him to the fatal tree; he was just about to affix the rope, when a tall yeoman leaped out of an adjacent bush, and with a stroke of his sword felled the officer to the earth.

"' I'm come to take leave of thee, Will, before thou diest,' cried the intruder; 'and, good master sheriff, thou must spare him to me awhile/"

"' As I live,' cried the sheriff, to his attendants, ' yon varlet's a rebel too, and one of Robin Hood's men, — seize him — five pounds for his head, dead or alive.' But, in a moment, Little John, for he it was, cut the bonds that secured his comrade, and snatching a sword from one of the soldiers, gave it him, shouting, ' Fight, Will, defend thyself, man—Help is near.— To the rescue — To the rescue.' — And turning back to back, the two outlaws gallantly parried the attacks of their assailants.

" ' To the rescue ! To the rescue !' echoed a host of voices from a neighbouring wood; and Robin Hood, with seven-score men, bounded across the green plain. A flight of arrows from their bows rattled upon the armour of the soldiers, and more than one stuck into the sheriff's robe.

" ' Away, my men, away!' cried he, flying to the castle for shelter. "Tis Robin Hood himself;' and the knowledge that the outlaw would especially choose him for a mark added wings to the speed of the valiant sheriff. His men — nothing loth to follow such an example, vied with each other in the race, so greatly to the amusement of the merry outlaws that they could not for laughter discharge an arrow in pursuit of them.

" ' I little thought, good master, to have seen thy face again,' said Will Stutely; ' and to thee, my bold comrade,' he added, addressing Little John, ' to thee I owe my best thanks. 'Twill be a long day ere Will Stutely forgets thy kindness.'

" ' May we ever thus support each other in danger,' said Robin Hood, loud enough for the whole band to hear him. ' But, my brave yeomen, we must away, or we shall have the whole nest of hornets about our ears;' and, with many a laugh at the sudden flight of the sheriff, and the glorious rescue of one of their favourite companions, the bold foresters plunged again into the woods and returned to Bar-nesdale, where they celebrated the joyful occasion with feasting and music, till the stars glittering through the topmost branches of the trees warned them that the hour of rest was at hand.

ROBIN HOOD AND THE BEGGAR.

"For some long time after this last daring adventure, Robin Hood and his men were so hotly pressed by the sheriff that it was with difficulty that they eluded the pursuit. Now concealing themselves in the recesses of a cavern, now in the thickest coverts of the forest, they were obliged almost daily to change their abode, until at last, tired of the incessant chase, the sheriff disbanded his forces and returned to Nottingham.

" When the outlaws were well assured of this, they quickly came back to their old haunts in Barnesdale and Sherwood, and pursued their usual course of life. One evening Robin Hood was roving through the woods, when he espied a sturdy-looking beggar, clad in an old patched cloak, come jogging along. In his hand he carried a thick oaken staff, with which

he assisted himself in walking, and round his neck a well-filled meal-bag was suspended by a broad leathern belt, while three steeple crowned hats placed within each other, sheltered his bald pate from the rain and snow.

" ' Stay, good friend,' said Robin Hood to him as they met; * thou seem'st in haste to-night.'

" ' I've far to go yet,' answered the beggar, still pushing onwards, 6 and should look foolish enough to get to my lodging house when all the supper's done/

"' Ay! ay!' returned Robin Hood, walking by his side. ' So long as thou fillest thine own mouth, thou carest but little about mine. Lend me some money, my friend, till we meet again. I've not dined yet, and my credit at the tavern is but indifferent.'

"' If thou fastest till I give thee money,' replied the mendicant, ' thou'lt eat nothing this year. Thou'rt a younger man than I am, and ought to work: ' and the old fellow pushed on still more briskly.

" ' Now, by my troth, thou'rt but a churl,' cried the outlaw. ' If thou hast but one farthing in thy pouch, 'tshall part company with thee before I go. Off with thy ragged cloak, and let's see what treasures it conceals, or I'll make a window in it with my good broad arrows.'

"' Dost think I care for wee bits of sticks like them *?' said the beggar, laughing; ' they're fit for nothing but skewers for a housewife's pudding-bag.' Robin Hood drew back a pace or two, and fitted an arrow to his bow-string, but before he could let it fly the beggar swung his staff round his head, and with one stroke splintered bow and arrow into twenty pieces. The outlaw drew his sword, and was about to repay this with interest, when a second blow from the old man's stick lighted upon his wrist, and so great was the pain it caused that his blade fell involuntarily from his grasp. Poor Robin Hood was now completely in the beggar's power; —

"' He could not fight — he could not flee, —
He wist not what to do; The heggar, with his nohle tree, Laid lusty slaps him to.

" ' He paid good Robin back and side,
And baste him up and down; And with his pike-staff laid on loud, Till he fell in a swoon.'

"' Stand up, man,' cried the beggar jeeringly, "tis hardly bed-time yet. Count thy money, man — buy ale and wine with it, and give thy friends a jovial carouse. How they'll laugh at the poor beggar.'

" Robin Hood answered not a word, but lay still as a stone ; his cheeks pale as ashes, and his eyes closed. The beggar gave him a parting thwack, and thinking that he had killed the saucy highwayman, went boldly on his way.

" It fortunately happened that Will Scarlet and two of his comrades were soon after passing by, and seeing a man lying by the road-side, apparently dead, walked up to him. What was their consternation and grief when they beheld their loved chief weltering in his blood. Will Scarlet bended upon one knee, and raised his master's head upon the other. One forester ran to a brook that flowed close by, and brought back his cap filled with water, which they sprinkled upon his face, and his companion drew from his pouch a little leathern bottle, the contents of which speedily revived the unfortunate outlaw.

" ' Tell us, dear master,' exclaimed Will Scarlet, ' who has done this ? '

" Robin Hood sighed deeply. ' I've roved in these woods for many years,' he said, 'but never have I been so hard beset as on this day. A beggar with an old patched cloak, for whom I would not have given a straw, has so basted my back with his pike-staff that it will be many a day ere Robin Hood will lead his merry men again.— See ! see !' he added as he raised his head; — ' there goes the man, on yonder hill, with three hats upon his head. My friends, — if you love your master, — go and revenge this deed; — bring him back to me, and let me see with mine own eyes the punishment youll give him.'

" ' One of us shall remain with thee,' replied Will; ' thou'rt ill at ease. The other two will quickly bring back yon evil-minded miscreant.'

"' Nay, nay,' returned the discomfited outlaw ; ' by my troth ye will have enough to do if he once get scope for that villanous staff of his.—Go, all of ye, — seize him suddenly — bind him fast, and bring him here, that 1 may repay him for these hard blows that he has given me.'

"Will Scarlet and his two companions started off as fast as they could run, dashing onward through many a miry pool, and over many a tiring hill, until they arrived at a part of the road that wound through the forest by a way at least a mile and a half nearer than the beaten path that the beggar had taken. There was a dense copse of trees in the bottom of a valley through which a little brook gently streamed, and the road-way ran close to it. The foresters, well acquainted with every acre of the ground which they so often traversed, took advantage of this grove, and concealed themselves behind the well covered branches. In the mean while the old beggar rejoicing in the victory he had so lately obtained, walked sturdily on, as briskly as age and his weary limbs would allow him. He passed by the copse without the least suspicion of lurking danger, but had proceeded only a step or two farther when his staff was violently seized by one of the foresters, and a dagger was pointed to his breast, with threats of vengeance if he resisted.

"' Oh! spare my life/ cried the beggar, at once relinquishing his hold, ' and take away that ugly knife. What have I done to deserve this *? I am but a poor beggar, who has never wronged thee or thine.'

" ' Thou liest, false carle/ replied Will, ' thou hast well nigh slain the noblest man that e'er trod the forest grass. Back shalt thou go to him, and before yon sun sinks down thy carcase shall be dangling from the highest tree in Barnesdale.'

" The beggar was sorely frightened at this terrible threat; he had lost his only weapon, and his aged limbs were but a poor match against three stout young men. He began to despair and to give himself up as lost, when a thought struck him. ' Brave gentlemen/ he said, ' why take ye a poor man's blood ? 'Twill make ye none the richer. If ye will give me liberty, and promise to do me no more harm, I have a hundred golden pounds in this meal-bag, that shall be yours.' The foresters whispered together and determined to get the money first, come afterwards what might.

" ' Give us thy money,' said Will, ' and we'll let thee go thy way.' The beggar unfastened the clasp of his belt, and taking it from his neck, spread the meal-bag upon the grass, while the young men anxious for the gold, bent over, eager to seize upon the expected prize. The old fellow pretended to search very diligently at the bottom of the bag, and pulled out a peck or two of meal, which he piled into a heap; then watch-

ing his opportunity, he filled both hands full, and threw it violently in the faces of the outlaws, who, blinded and astonished, began to rub their eyes most woefully. The beggar sprung up in a moment, seized his staff, and in a twinkling began to belabour their backs and shoulders.

" 4 1 have mealed your coats,' he cried, ' but I've a good pike-staff here that will soon beat them clean again;' and before the youths could recover from their consternation the old man plied his staff so manfully that his arm ached from the exertion, and he was obliged to stay for rest.

" The young outlaws did not attempt to retaliate; indeed they could not see where to strike; but trusting to their swiftness, scampered away even more briskly than they had come; and the beggar laughing at the success of his wile, plunged into the woods, and made the best of his way from Barnesdale forest.

" When Will Scarlet and his comrades presented themselves before Robin Hood, the bold outlaw, ill as he was, could not refrain from bursting into laughter at their sheepish appearance. They hung down their heads, and still rubbed their eyes, while the meal on

their coats made known the trick that had been played upon them.

" 'What have ye done with the bold beggar 4 ?' inquired Kobin Hood; c surely three of ye were a match for him.' Will Scarlet replied; told him of their first success, and the old man's promise of money ; but when he came to the meal and the drubbing they had received, Robin Hood laughed till his bruised limbs ached. Although he would fain have revenged himself upon his opponent, yet the cleverness of the trick so pleased his fancy that he swore that if ever he met the sturdy beggar again, he would, by fair means or foul, make him join his band in merry Barnesdale."

This tale was frequently interrupted with the loud laughter of my hearers, who all praised the dexterity of the old beggar-man.

THE THIRD EVENING.
THE OUTLAWS' SPORTS.

UPON the next evening that we met together I found my school-fellows waiting for me under the old tree, and taking my usual seat, I immediately began: —

" Many a gay meadow bedecked with daisies and buttercups stretches its verdant surface by the banks of the fair river Trent; and many a wood filled with merry birds lines its brink so closely that the pendent branches of the trees lave themselves in its transparent waters. It was upon the evening of a lovely day in spring, when every flower looked fresh and beautiful, and the early leaves of the forest shone in their brightest green tint, that a party of young men emerging upon one of these meadows from the surrounding woods, began to amuse themselves in the athletic exercises in which our forefathers so much delighted. Some of them struck slight branches into the earth, and placing a pole transversely upon them, leaped over it at nearly their own height from the ground. Presently a signal was given, and four or five youths bounded across the lawn with the speed of young stags, vieing with each other in the first attainment of the solitary elm that graced the centre of the meadow. High swelled the bosom of the victor as, breathless and panting, he received the reward of his achievement, perhaps a new scarlet cap, or a bright new girdle, and proud was he to know that the chief to whom he had sworn allegiance beheld and smiled approvingly on his success.

"But now a more important contest began. One of the foresters stood forward, and fixed up a target, the face of which was rudely painted in circles of various colours, a small white spot serving as a centre. A line was drawn at the distance of five hundred feet from this mark, near which about twenty bowmen took their station; one after another each stept up to it, bent his bow, and let fly an arrow with all the force he could command. Many shafts had flown far wide of the target, and some few had struck it near

the side, when the turn arrived for a gaily-dressed archer to make his trial. Walking deliberately to the line, he very carefully placed his arrow upon the bowstring, raised it till it was on a level with his ear, and instantly discharged it. The quivering shaft sank deeply within two inches of the white centre.

" ' Bravely done, Will Scarlet,' exclaimed a forester who stood apart from the rest, and who evidently controlled their movements; ' thou'lt soon become as good a bowman as e'er trod the green-wood.'

"'I do my best, good master,' replied Will to Robin Hood, who had taken advantage of the cool evening, in order to exercise his men; ' but here is one whom I fear I scarcely equal:' and a bold forester, who was known to his companions by the cognomen of ' Much, the Miller's Son,' stood forward, and drew his bow. The nicely-balanced arrow shot swift as lightning through the air, and pierced the very centre of the target. A loud huzza followed this achievement, and Robin Hood himself shouted louder than the rest. In a moment after all was hushed, for the tall forester, brave Little John, took the last turn, and his comrades, knowing well his dexterity, F breathlessly awaited the result of the contest. After carefully selecting a well-feathered arrow, he stood erect as a young tree, drew back his bow-string with the strength of a giant, and suddenly let it slip. For a minute or two no one could tell where the arrow had gone; it was just possible to trace its flight as it whizzed through the air, but it was not to be seen on the target. Little John, smiling as he beheld the looks of surprise, ran swiftly across the intervening space, and, to their astonishment, drew forth his shaft from out of that of the miller's, which it had struck, and cloven about half way down.

" Robin Hood and his followers shouted with rapture, and the victor bending upon one knee, received from his master, as a reward for his prowess, a beautiful arrow of silver.

"' By my troth,' said the outlaw, as he gave it to him, ' I would ride a hundred miles, any day, to find an archer like thee.'

" ' Thou'st no need to go so far,' cried Will Scarlet, rather envious of the better success of his companions. ' There's a friar in Fountains' Dale that will bend a bow against him or thee, ay, or against all thy men.'

" ' I'll neither eat nor drink till I find him,' said the bold outlaw. ' Tis too late to seek him this evening, but ere I break my fast to-morrow I'll see this valiant friar.' And as he spake he drew an arrow from his quiver, and fixed it upon his bow-string.

" A young hart had innocently trotted forth from the shelter of the woods, and was making its way towards the brink of the river, when the noise of the foresters reached its ear. Startled at the sound, the creature turned its pretty head, gazed for a moment, and, frightened at the unaccustomed scene, bounded at full speed back towards the concealment of the forest. The outlaw's keen eye had followed its motions, and wishing to display the superiority of his skill, he let fly an arrow at it while in its swiftest flight; the poor fawn immediately dropped, although the distance between it and the archer was, at the least, a quarter of a mile.

" ' Dost think the friar of Fountains' Abbey will beat that*?' asked Robin Hood as he slackened his bow-string.

" ' Ay marry, that will he,' replied Will Scarlet; 4 many's the buck he has killed at half a mile.'

" ' I'll never draw bow again,' returned the chief, ' if F 2 a lazy friar once beats me in archery. What say ye, my friends, shall we find out this gallant priest ? '

" ' Make him join us/ cried several voices.

" ' To-morrow at earliest dawn be ready to attend me/ said Robin Hood; and with Little John by his side, he left the meadow.

" The foresters then parted into groups and strolled away, some to the banks of the stream, others to the darkening woods, while a few, not yet content as ta their inferiority, sought again to try their speed against the victors.

ROBIN HOOD AND THE FRIAR.

" Upon the next morning, ere the sun had risen above the horizon, Robin Hood started from his couch, and armed himself. He put on his helmet and breast-plate, he took up his good broadsword, his long tried buckler, and his trustiest bow, and then placing his bugle-horn to his lips, he played so loud a reveille that his men, frightened from their slumbers, seized their nearest weapons, as if an army had appeared against them. A few gentler notes made them remember the appointed time, and soon fifty bold youths attended the summons of their master. He bade them hasten to Fountains', Dale by the shortest path, but on no account to show themselves till he had sounded three blasts upon his bugle; and with a light foot and merry heart he sprang into his horse's saddle, and set out to encounter the renowned friar.

" This friar, whose fame was spread far and wide, had once been an inmate and one of the brethren of Fountains' Abbey, but his irregular course of life and lawless pursuits had brought down upon him the wrath of the superior, and he had been expelled. Friar Tuck, so was he called, bore his disgrace boldly; he immediately retired to the forests, and there built himself a rude hut of the large stones with which the country abounded, thatching it with branches of trees. There he lived hi solitude, gaining from the country people, who frequently came to him for religious consolation, a character of the greatest sanctity. The friar took care to turn this to his advantage, and many were the presents of butter, milk, and sometimes of a more enlivening liquid, that he received. But these did not constitute his chief means of livelihood; early in the morning the friar had more than once been seen with a good long bow in his hand, and a quiver of arrows at his side, and a report had gone abroad that few could equal him in the use of this favourite weapon.

" The friar was a tall burly man, at least six feet high, with a broad expanded chest, and a muscular arm that the sturdiest blacksmith might have been proud of. He usually wore a dark mulberry coloured cloak that reached nearly to his ancles, and girded it with a black woollen rope, the two ends of which hung down before him, about half a yard in length. On the morning upon which Robin Hood had determined to discover him, from some unaccountable reason friar Tuck had put a steel cap upon his head, and a corslet upon his breast, and with his long oaken staff in his hand had rambled to the margin of the fair river Skell, where he stood gazing steadfastly upon the waves, as they rippled by. Presently he heard the sound of a horse's step, and turning, he beheld within a few feet of him an armed horseman. The stranger quickly dismounted, and fastening his steed by his bridle, to the branch of a tree, advanced towards him.

" ' Art thou the Friar of Fountains' Abbey ? ' he asked, when each had regarded the other in silence for a short space.

" ' They that speak of me call me so,' replied the priest; ' why dost thou seek me ? '

"'Carry me over this stream, thou burly friar, and I will tell thee,' replied Robin Hood. The priest, without a word, tucked up his garments to the waist, took the daring outlaw upon his back, and gravely waded across the stream. Robin Hood leaped off lightly upon the opposite bank.

" ' Now do thou carry me back, thou gay gallant/ said the friar. The outlaw stooped, took him upon his shoulders, and with great difficulty bore his weighty burden across.

"'Now by my faith thou'rt double the weight that I am,' cried Robin Hood as the priest alighted, 4 and I'll have two rides to thy one.' The friar did not answer, but taking up the merry forester again, bore him to the middle of the stream, and bending down, pitched him headlong into the water.

"' Choose thee, my fine fellow, whether thou'lt

sink or swim!' he said; ' a morning bath will do thine health good.' Robin Hood scrambled to the bank, fitted an arrow to his bow, and let it fly at the treacherous friar; but the wet had sodden both the bowstring and the feathers of the shaft, and it flew far wide. The priest not wishing to stand a second trial, flourished his staff and knocked the bow from the grasp of the forester, who quickly drew his sword and retaliated by severely wounding his vigorous opponent upon the shoulder. The friar at this grew wrathful, and returned a most terrible thwack upon the outlaw's head. Blow followed upon blow; now the thick oaken staff beat down the less weighty but more deadly weapon, and again the sharp edge of the sword drank blood. They fought thus for more than an hour, and each began to weary of such warm work before breakfast.

'"A boon, a boon,' cried Robin Hood, retiring from the contest. 'Give me leave to sound three blasts upon my bugle-horn.'

"' Blow till thy cheeks crack,' returned the friar. ' Think'st thou I fear a bugle blast ?' The outlaw sounded the horn thrice, so loudly that the friar

ROBIN HOOD &, THE, FRIAR.

clapped his hands to his ears, and beat a retreat for several yards. The signal was immediately returned, and apparently from close at hand. In two minutes more a tall yeoman leaped from the adjacent wood> and followed by fifty young foresters, with bows ready in their hands, ran to the side of their commander.

"' Whose men are these $' asked the friar, greatly surprised at this sudden reinforcement.

"' They're Kobin Hood's bold foresters,' said the outlaw; ' and I am Robin Hood. Wilt join our merry troop ? Thou'rt the bravest friar that e'er wore cowl, and if thou canst let fly an arrow as well as thou canst wield a quarter-staff, thou'rt a match for my boldest man.'

"' Let's have a bout,' said friar Tuck, unwilling to fight against such odds as were opposed to him. ' If there's an archer here that can beat me at the longbow, I'll be thy man. If I'm the best, swear that thou wilt leave me free in mine own woods.'

"' Agreed!' cried the outlaw. ' Stand forth, brave Little John, and for the credit of Robin Hood choose thy truest shaft.'

"' Ne'er fear me/ replied the tall forester, as he carelessly advanced. ' Shoot on, my brave fellow, and at what mark you may, only for St. Hubert's sake, let it be some five hundred feet or so from us.'

"' Seest thou yon bird ? ' said the friar, pointing to a hawk that, with fluttering wings, hovered at a considerable height above a neighbouring brake. ' I will kill it. If thou canst strike it again ere it reaches the earth, I'll say thou art a better man than friar Tuck.' Drawing an arrow from his quiver, with apparent ease he shot the ill-fated bird, which instantly fell to the earth, but not before a second shaft had transfixed its body. A young forester darted away, and quickly returned with the prize, when it appeared that the friar's arrow had pinioned the hawk's wings to its sides, and that Little John's had pierced through from its breast to its back.

"' Well done, my brave archers/ cried the outlaws' chief; 'there's many a bowman in merry England would give his best weapon to shoot like ye. What says my gallant friar *? will he keep his promise "? '

"' What I have said, that will I do,' replied the priest; ' but first I must return to my hut, and possess myself of its valuable contents/ Kobin Hood offered to accompany him, and dismissing his followers, he and the friar by turns rode upon the horse, first to the hut and then to the green woods of Sherwood.

ROBIN HOOD AND THE BISHOP OF HEREFORD.

" Robin Hood used frequently to disguise himself, and pay visits to the neighbouring villages, in order to learn if any thing were going on in which he might take a part. In one of these excursions, he overheard a conversation between two priests, by which he learned that the bishop of Hereford was expected to pass that way very shortly, upon a visit to his holy brother, the archbishop of York. The outlaw lost no time in ascertaining the route which the reverend father would travel, and with a merry heart he hurried back to his followers in Sherwood forest. At the sound of his well known bugle, two-score yeomen quickly surrounded him, Little John and Will Scarlet among them.

"' We shall have noble company to dine with us,' said Robin Hood. ' Kill a good fat buck or two, and prepare a feast.' Three or four foresters quickly darted away to execute this commission.

"' Who may it be, master,' asked Little John, ' that loves to be merry under the green-wood tree *?'

" ' Love or not love,' cried the captain laughing, ' a holy bishop dines with us to-day, though he brings a dozen companions with him. But 'tis time to meet his reverence. Do thou and Will Scarlet attend me, and thou too, — and thou, — and thou,' — he added, tapping with his bow the heads of three of his tallest followers, who most willingly and joyfully complied.

" The bishop of Hereford, as many bishops were in those days, was very rich, very avaricious, and exceedingly tyrannical. By the nobles he was regarded as a powerful prelate, and a support to the dignity of the church; but the people looked upon him with fear, as a proud, overbearing priest. Upon the occasion of his visit to his brother of York, the bishop of Hereford rode on horseback, dressed in the white robes of his sacred office; a massive gold chain was suspended round his neck, supporting a golden crucifix, and in his right hand he carried his crosier, of the same precious metal. His milk-white steed, also, was richly caparisoned with silken trappings. The dean of Hereford, attired in a plain black cassock, rode humbly by the side of his superior, who, from time to time, deigned to hold converse with him upon the vanities of this wicked world. Behind them, twenty horsemen, armed at all points, with broadswords by their sides and lances in rest, followed slowly upon chargers of the jettest black, and three or four servants leading sumpter mules closed the rear. Notwithstanding all this pompous array, it was with many a misgiving that the bishop ventured to enter upon the dangerous road through Sherwood forest.

"' Holy brother,' said he to the dean, c dost thou think that the man called Robin Hood will dare to molest the Lord's anointed, if perchance he should have heard of our journeying*? '

"'They say, reverend father,' replied the dean, 'that he holds the holy brethren of the church but cheaply, and pays but little respect to any of our cloth. I would that we had taken a more circuitous route, and avoided the paths of this wicked man.'

"' It is too late to return now,' said the bishop; ' and have we not twenty armed men to support us in the hour of trial! — Comfort ye, my brother,— with this

will I drive off the enemies of holy church;' and as he spake he flourished his crosier above his head. They had proceeded but a short way farther, when they suddenly came upon six shepherds, dancing merrily round a fire, with which they were cooking venison, by the road-side.

"' Ha!' cried the bishop when he smelt the savoury odour that exhaled from the roasting flesh. ' Dare ye, villains as ye are, slay the king's deer, and cook it upon the open road 4 ? By St. Paul, ye shall answer for this.'

"' Mercy! mercy! good bishop,' cried one of the shepherds; c surely it beseemeth not thy holy office to take away the lives of so many innocent peasants.'

" ' Guards, seize these villains/ cried the prelate, indignant at the presumption of the serf; — 'away with them to York,— they shall be strung on the highest gibbet in the city.' The armed horsemen turned not over-willingly against the offenders, and endeavoured to seize them, but with a loud laugh they darted among the trees, where the steeds could not possibly follow. Presently the shepherd who had begged for mercy pulled from under his frock a little

bugle-horn, and blew a short call upon it. The bishop and his retinue started with affright, and had already begun to urge on their horses, when they found themselves surrounded on every side by archers, dressed in green, with bows drawn in their hands.

" * Mercy ! mercy !' cried the bishop in great trepidation at the sight of fifty or more arrows ready to pierce him through. ' Have mercy upon an unfortunate traveller/

"Tear not, good father,' replied Robin Hood, who was the shepherd that had before spoken; ' we do but crave thy worshipful company to dine with us under the green-wood tree, and then, when thou hast paid the forest toll, thou shalt depart in safety ;' and, stepping into the road, the bold outlaw laid one hand upon the embossed bridle of the bishop's steed, and held the stirrup with the other.

"' Oh! that we had but gone the outer road,' groaned the bishop to his holy brother; ' we should have avoided these limbs of the evil one/

"' Nay, nay reverend father,' cried Robin Hood, laughing at the poor bishop's rueful countenance; ' call us not by so bad a name. We do but take from the rich to administer to the necessities of the poor and if we do now and then slay a fat buck or two, our good king will never know his loss. But dismount, holy sir; and do ye, my friends, come likewise; right merry shall we be with such a jovial company.' The horsemen quickly did as they were bidden, but the bishop most reluctantly unseated himself, and with many a deep sigh obeyed the injunction of the outlaw. Some of the foresters immediately seized the horses, and tied their bridles to the lower branches of the trees; but the sumpter mules were hurried away through the wood as quickly as the narrow foot-paths would allow.

" At Eobin Hood's command, two young fellows took the unwilling bishop between them upon their shoulders, and followed by the whole company, bore him to their favourite lawn. A solitary beech tree, whose arms, covered with thick foliage, extended far around, stood in the centre, affording a delightful shade from the bright summer sun. Robin Hood seated himself upon one of the twisted roots that grew above the surface of the turf, and commanded that his visitor should be brought before him. Little John, taking off his cap as he approached, gently led him to the outlaw, while, to show his spite against him, one of the young foresters had the audacity to tie the prelate's arms behind his back.

"' Thou art accused of deep crimes,' exclaimed Robin Hood. ' It is said that thou dost gripe the poor man with a hard hand, and showest but little mercy to the unfortunate. How answerest thou ? '

"' By what right, mean serf,' replied the bishop, the blood rushing to his temples, ' dost thou question an anointed servant of the church *? '

"' Pax vobiscum,' cried friar Tuck, coming forward, and folding his arms in an attitude of defiance. ' Wherefore not, good father *? Answer boldly, and swear by St. Paul that thou ne'er robbed the fatherless and the widow.'

u * What canting priest art thou ? ' exclaimed the bishop. 'For thine insolence thou shalt be expelled the church; thy gown shall be stripped from thee, and thou shalt be branded as an impostor/

"' Save thyself the trouble,' replied the friar, laughing. « The holy abbot of Fountains' Dale has forestalled thee in thy kind intentions.'

G

"' Hold,' cried Kobin Hood, rising from his seat, ' we'll have no more of these priestly quarrels. Reve-rend father, accompany us to our trysting tree, and we'll drink to thy speedy amendment.' Then cutting his bonds with a dagger, he took the hand of his unwilling guest, and led him to the spot where they usually partook of their repasts.

" Upon the grass was spread a large cloth, covered with viands. Smoking haunches of venison perfumed the air, and huge pasties baked in pewter vessels, roasted wild swans, peacocks, and a host of minor dishes, filled up any vacancies upon the cloth. At Robin Hood's request, the bishop said grace, and fifty or more foresters quickly seated themselves to partake of this gallant feast. The prelate, for one in his situation, ate most heartily. His merry host no sooner saw that his platter was empty than he again filled it from the most savoury dishes. Wine flowed in abundance, and when, in obedience to Robin Hood, every man filled his goblet to the brim, and quaffed its contents to the health of the bishop of Hereford, the good father for some moments quite forgot his misfortunes, and striking

THE BISHOP OF HEREFORD.
his palm into the sinewy hand of Robin Hood, swore that he was a jovial fellow.

" Many a ballad was then trolled forth by the foresters, and in the excitement of the scene even the bishop ventured upon a stave; but, at the moment he had concluded the first verse, his eye caught sight of one of his mules, from whose back an outlaw was busily removing the trunk that contained his treasure.

"' Bring me the reckoning, good host/ said he meekly, stopping short in his song; ' I would fain discharge it, and proceed upon my journey.'

" ' Lend me thy purse, good bishop,' cried Little John, ' and I will save thee the trouble.'

"' Take it,' replied the prelate, throwing a very light bag of money to the forester, 'and give the surplus to the poor.'

" Little John opened the mouth of the purse, and emptied out ten golden nobles upon the grass. 'And dost thou think,' he exclaimed, laughing heartily at the owner's rueful countenance, —' dost thou think that a bishop pays no more toll than this"? Verily, reverend father, the meanest farmer in Nottingham-shire readily grants us so poor a trifle. Ho there!' he cried to the man who was disburdening the mules, 'bring hither yonder trunk.' It was quickly brought, and with the help of a broadsword soon opened. Little John first pulled out a handsome cloak, which he spread upon the grass ; a gown of the purest white lawn, an ermined robe, and a golden mitre, were each brought forth in succession, and greatly admired by the delighted foresters; but presently a clink of metal was heard, and the bold robber drew forth a beautiful ivory casket. The point of a dagger was in a moment applied to the fastening, and treasures invaluable were revealed. The bishop, who had sat shivering with anxiety during the search, now suddenly sprang to his feet with wonderful alacrity, and would have seized his precious wealth, had not Robin Hood caught him by the arm.

" ' Calm thyself, good father,' said the outlaw; ' do but fancy that thou art distributing this gold in alms to the poor, and thou wilt ne'er repent thee of thy charity.' The bishop did not reply, but gazed steadfastly on the glittering coin, the sparkling jewels,

and the holy beads, that Little John was exhibiting to his companions.

"' Rouse ye, my merry men,' cried the chief; ' see ye not how sad ye have made our reverend guest!' A young man quickly brought a rude harp, upon which he struck a lively air, and the gallant outlaw taking the bishop by the hand, led him forth, followed by the foresters in pairs. The dance commenced, and the poor prelate, unwilling to provoke his tormentors to extremities, joined in the nimble step, which was prolonged till his weary feet could no longer sustain their burden. The,reverend father fell fairly to the earth from sheer exhaustion.

"At Robin Hood's bidding, the two young men again took the bishop upon their shoulders, and bore him to the spot where his steed and those of his retinue were fastened. They placed him upon his saddle, with his face to the animal's tail, and giving it him instead of the bridle, they pricked the creature with their daggers, and started it off at full gallop, the terrified rider clinging both with hands and knees to its back. The dean, the armed horse-

men, and the servants were allowed to follow their superior in peace; but the sumpter mules and their burdens were detained as payment for the feast that had been given to their owners."

OUR HALF-HOLIDAY.
THE WOOD.

IT was, I remember, upon a Saturday afternoon that I was again asked to tell a tale of Robin Hood. On this, the last day of our week of seclusion, how great were -the pleasures of our half-holiday! Frequently we had permission granted us to stroll among the fields in the neighbourhood; in the spring time, to gather the bright yellow primrose, or search for the nests of the poor innocent birds; and, in the autumn season, to pluck the delicious blackberries that, in some places, — and we knew them well, — abounded among the thorny hedges.

At about the distance of a quarter of a mile from our old school-house there was an extensive park. Many hundred acres of land were covered with fine trees — oaks, elms, and firs, variously intermixed — while here and there were open lawns, clothed only

with grass and the beautiful wild flowers, that spring up, unnurtured, in their native soil. An ancient mansion stood in the midst, upon the summit of a hill, whence, looking over the woods, the face of the country for miles around could be traced as upon a map. The house was deserted—the owner resided in a foreign land, and his noble English park was neglected: it had once been paled round, but in many places the wooden staves were broken, and a gap made, through which every passenger might enter. We often did, and chased each other among the crowded thickets; and now, glad of the opportunity of escaping from our confined play-ground, we repaired to this delightful park, where, seated upon the grass, with my companions lying around me, I told them the tale of

ROBIN HOOD IN FINSBURY FIELD.

" In the time of Henry the Second, and for many years afterwards, until the use of gunpowder was known, the science of archery was greatly encouraged in England among all ranks and classes ; and even the good citizens of London constantly exercised their bows in ' Finsburie fielde.'

"The feast of St. Bartholomew was particularly celebrated by games of this kind: a finely wrought bow or a golden arrow was given as a prize to the best marksman, and the presence of the king and his court contributed not a little to add interest to the long looked-for contests.

" One year, towards the close of King Henry's reign, proclamation was as usual made, that the ' royal games of archery' would be held in Finsbury field, upon St. Bartholomew's day. Queen Eleanor was passionately fond of the sport, and rarely missed an opportunity of witnessing the superior skill displayed by the royal archers. She had heard much of Kobin Hood, but had never seen that gallant outlaw; and as the fame of his rencontre with the bishop of Hereford had spread far and wide, she felt a secret desire to behold so daring and so celebrated a man. Summoning a young page who waited her commands, she gave him a beautiful golden ring, and bade him hasten with all speed to Sherwood forest, and deliver it to the forester, with her request that he would come to London and take a part in the approaching games. The youth lost no time in executing his mistress'

command, and in two days arrived at Nottingham, where, from a good yeoman, he learned the dwelling-place of Eobin Hood, and on the next morning he appeared before the bold outlaw. Falling gracefully upon one knee, he doffed his cap, and presented the ring to him^ saying, —' My royal and most gracious mistress, Eleanor, queen of England, greets thee well. She bids thee haste with all speed to fair London court, that thou may'st be her champion in the sports upon the feast of St. Bartholomew, in token whereof accept this ring/

" The outlaw took the royal present, and placed it upon his finger. ' Rise, my pretty page/ he said; ' wend thou back upon the fleetest steed that thou canst find. Deliver this arrow to Queen Eleanor, and say that Robin Hood will claim it ere three suns have set.' The young page rose, placed the arrow in his belt, and with much courtesy bade the outlaw adieu; then hastening to his inn at Nottingham, he chose the swiftest horse in the stables, and flew back again to his royal mistress.

" Early in, the morning of St. Bartholomew's day, Finsbury field presented a gay and most enlivening scene. The large open space, which then existed where streets and squares are now crowded together, was covered with the good citizens of London and their wives and daughters, bedecked in their newest holiday costume. Lists, three hundred yards in length, were marked out in the centre of the field, and railed round, to prevent the entrance of the spectators. At one end a scaffold was erected for the accommodation of the king and queen and their attendants; it was hung with green silk, emblazoned with the royal arms in gold, and covered over with a beautiful bright blue cloth, spangled with silver stars. Near it were tents pitched for the use of the contending bowmen, and immediately opposite, at the far end of the lists, a broad target was placed, with a large wooden screen behind it, to stop the flight of any stray arrows that did not hit the mark. All were in busy expectation, — for the royal party had not yet arrived, — and many were the wagers laid upon the favourite archers of Finsbury. At length a blast of trumpets was heard, and two heralds, dressed in glittering coats of golden tissue, with emblazoned banners hanging from their spirit-stirring instruments, entered the ground. The

mounted on a barbed charger, and the queen upon a milk-white palfrey, both magnificently caparisoned, then appeared, amid the waving of caps, and the deafening acclamations of the assembled thousands. Next followed, upon steeds of the purest white, a bevy of fair ladies in attendance upon their royal mistress; and a band of knights and gentlemen, well mounted and richly dressed, closed the procession.

"As soon as the royal party I had alighted, and had taken their seats upon the gallery, proclamation was made by sound of trumpet, that a tun of the best Rhenish wine, and a hundred of the fattest harts that ran in ; Dallom Chase,' would be given to the truest marksman. The archers were then ordered to advance to their posts, and a line was drawn upon which they were to step when they discharged their arrows. Six bowmen appeared, wearing the king's livery, and marching to the gallery, they doffed their caps to their royal master, and took their appointed station.

" ' Is there no one,' asked King Henry aloud, —4s there no bold forester to oppose my gallant archers ?'

"' A boon, my liege, — a boon,'— cried Queen Eleanor. ' Promise me by the saint whose feast we celebrate, that whoever draws bow on my side shall depart uninjured and free for forty days.'

" ' I grant thy boon, fair Eleanor,' replied the king ; ' but who are these gallant bowmen that require thine intercession*?'

" ' Bid the heralds sound again,' said Eleanor, ' and thou shalt see them.' The trumpets again played, and the challenge from the king's archers was repeated.

" The queen waved a light green scarf, and six tall yeomen entered the lists, and advancing to the gallery, bowed lowly to their royal patroness. One of them, evidently the commander of the little band, was clothed in a rich scarlet doublet and tnmk hose of the same bright colour; a baldric of light blue silk, interwoven with threads of gold, crossed his shoulder, supporting his quiver and a small golden bugle, and in his hand he carried a most beautifully wrought bow. His companions were dressed in the favourite Lincoln green, and like their commander, each wore a black bonnet with a white streaming feather.

" 'Welcome, good Locksley,' said the queen, addressing the yeoman in scarlet. 'Thou must draw thy

94 THE ROYAL GAMES OF ARCHERY.

best bow for Queen Eleanor ;' then turning to the noblemen around her, ' Who will support our brave party $' she asked. ' My good lord bishop of Hereford, wilt thou not in gallantry be on our side *? '

" ' Thou hast six of the best archers of Finsbury to contend against, gracious madam,' replied the prelate, ' and thy men are all strangers; we know not if they can draw a bowstring.'

"' Will your grace wager against us *?' asked Locksley of the bishop.

" ' Aye! by my mitre, willingly,' returned the bishop rather warmly; ' I'll wager a purse of gold against thee and thy whole band;' and he drew forth about fifty golden nobles. Locksley replied by throwing upon the turf before the gallery a little bag containing at least an equal quantity of the precious metal, and both stakes were given to the king as umpire of the sport.

" The royal archers now took their station upon the line, and one after another let fly an arrow at the broad target. 'Why give us such a mark as •that'?' cried one of them, named Clifton, as his arrow pierced the centre. 'We'll shoot at the sun and moon.

' Boldly said, my fine fellow,' replied Locksley as he drew his bowstring; ' you and I will have a bout together presently:' and carelessly discharging his arrow, it quivered within a hair's breadth of his opponent's. The spectators pleased at such fine archery, shouted at the sight, but the king and the bishop of Hereford could ill conceal their surprise and disappointment. Locksley's men followed, and each one's arrow alighted within a few inches of the centre of the target, but so had those of the royal archers.

" ' The game is equal,' said the king, when he had mounted his horse and galloped across the field; 'ye must shoot again, my brave men. Finsbury has ne'er before seen such archery as this.'

" ' If my gallant friend here,' cried Locksley, ' who aims at nothing less than bringing down yon glorious sun, will but agree to the trial, he and I might decide this contest between ourselves. That is,' he continued, ' with your majesty's royal leave.'

'"What say'st thou, Clifton? art thou content to stake thy reputation against this braggart's *?' asked King Henry.

" ' Right willingly, my liege,' replied the archer;

' I'll lay my own trusty bow against his, that he hits not the mark that I do.*

"'A fair wager,' cried Locksley, 'which I readily accept.'

" At the instigation of the champions the broad target was removed, and in its place, a slight willow wand, not above an inch and a half in circumference, was planted firmly in the earth. The spectators gazed with increased wonder. ' They surely will not aim at such a mark as that,' said they one to another. But the royal bowman stepped to the line, and after carefully adjusting his arrow, let it fly: it peeled off the bark of the wand as it passed by, and alighted in the earth a few yards farther on. A loud huzza rent the air, and ' Clifton! a Clifton!' was shouted from one end of the lists to the other. The gay yeoman did not wait till these cries had subsided. c I will notch his shaft,' he said aloud as he advanced composedly to his post; and fitting his arrow, he drew the bowstring to his ear, and after one moment's deliberation discharged the weapon with his utmost force. The shaft flew true, and to the amazement of the beholders, rived asunder that of his

opponent. At first a deep silence prevailed, many could not see where the arrow had struck, and some were dumb with astonishment; but when one of the attendants pulled it forth, a shout of applause was raised, so loud, so long, and so vehement, that those of the good citizens of London who had remained at home rushed forth from the gates in hundreds to inquire the cause of so violent an outbreak.

"The king's vexation at this defeat of his party quickly changed into admiration of Locksley's superior skill. He rode up to his side : ' Wilt thou be one of my archers 2' he asked ; ' a hundred pounds a year, the free use of my pantry, and a new suit of livery each three months, shall be thy reward.'

"' It grieves me, my liege,' replied the yeoman, 'that I cannot comply with thy request; but grant me one boon, and I and my gallant men will support thee to our deaths.'

" ' Name it, good Locksley ; 'tis already granted;' said the king.

"' Pardon, most gracious liege, pardon for the outlawed Robin Hood and his brave followers.'

"' And art thou Robin Hood *?' asked Henry, H

his countenance flushed with anger, c whose defiance of the law has filled the whole north country with alarm. By St. George, but thou art the boldest villain that e'er shot bow. Ho! guards there, take charge of this over-valiant knave.'

"' Remember thy promise,' cried a gentle voice from the gallery. 'Remember thou hast pledged thine honour.

"King Henry turned as he recognised the sweet tones of his lovely consort, and a smile played upon his lips as he replied, "Twas but in jest, fair Eleanor, ' twas but in jest.' ' We will willingly grant pardon to thee and thy followers,' he continued to the outlaw, ' if ye will forsake your unlawful pursuits, and lead the sober lives of honest yeomen.'

" c We cannot quit the green woods of Sherwood,' said Robin Hood; 'but if your majesty will grant us leave to range the forest, and now and then exercise our archery upon one of the thousands of fat deer that bound so gaily o'er the lawns, we will promise that no traveller shall again complain of the outlaws of Nottinghamshire.'

"The king bit his lips in silence, but at that moment the defeated archer advanced and tendered his bow to the victor.

"' Thou'rt a good marksman, Clifton,' said he ; ' if thou hadst made a little more allowance for the distance, thine arrow would not have passed the wand ; keep thy bow, man; though I tell it thee, there's but one better archer in merry England.'

"' If I had known that thou wert Robin Hood,' cried the bishop of Hereford, as the king delivered the well-filled purses to the outlaw, ' I would not have wagered against thee. Thou hast already had more gold of mine than I e'er intended.'

"' Surely thou dost not forget the jovial dinner we gave thee under our trysting tree,' replied Robin Hood; ' yet if thou dost begrudge the payment, I will return it even now.'

"'Nay, nay, master,' cried Little John, who had accompanied his captain, ' that were unwise; since thou hast promised not to relieve travellers of their superfluous wealth, 'twere folly not to keep all the gold thou comest honestly by.' Robin Hood with a smile threw the purses to his more considerate follower, bowed low to the king, and still lower to his fair patroness, and accompanied by his five gay yeomen, departed from the field.

" Sherwood forest soon rung again with the sound of his bugle-horn, but the promise given on Finsbury field was kept during King Henry's life-time; no traveller had reason to complain of the bold outlaws.

THE KNIGHT OF WIERYSDALE.

" We must suppose that several years had elapsed since Robin Hood's victory in Finsbury field, when the following tale commences. Richard the Lion-hearted had succeeded to his father's throne, and with many of his nobles had joined the memorable crusades. During his absence in Palestine, the internal state of England had become far worse than it was at the time of his accession. Baron rose up against baron, and princes made war upon each other, till discord, tumult, and fierce rapine, reigned throughout the land. It was not, therefore, to be wondered at, when the laws were for a time suspended and force of arms alone decided the contest, that the bold foresters had again recourse to their superior strength.

"It was a bright morning in early summer, when a solitary horseman was proceeding upon his journey through one of the narrow roads that crossed Barnes-dale forest ;

"' All dreary was his semblance,
And little was his pride, His one foot in the stirrup stood, The other waved beside;

"' His hood was hanging o'er his eyes,

He rode in simple array, A sorrier man than he was one Rode never on summer's day.'

•" A deep sigh escaped from the melancholy horseman, and big tears coursed each other down his cheeks, at every step of his poor lean beast; and when three men suddenly emerged from the wood, and stood before his path, he seemed scarcely conscious of their presence.

"' God save thee, sir knight, 7 cried one of them, a tall' forester, nearly seven feet high, moved with compassion at his forlorn appearance. 'Welcome to our merry green-wood. Thou must be our guest to-day.'

"'Leave me, good sirs, I pray ye,' said the knight mournfully, 'my sorrows are already too heavy for me to bear; add not to my distress.'

"' Nay, be not so downcast,' returned the former speaker. c Thou art in good hands, and may'st trust us. Our master waits dinner for a guest, and thou art the first man who has passed through Barnesdale this day.' Then taking the knight's rein in his hand, the forester led the jaded steed through the intricate paths of the wood, until he arrived at an open lawn, where a band of yeomen were reclining under the shade of a huge elm.

" ' Welcome, sir knight,' said one of them rising and doffing his cap at the appearance of a stranger. ' Welcome to merry Barnesdale.'

" Who art thou,' inquired the horseman, ' that causest travellers to be constrained from their way"? I am but a poor knight, without so much as a piece of gold, wherewith to buy me food.'

" ' More welcome still,' exclaimed the forester, assisting him from his horse. ' We shall have the blessings of charity upon our deeds. Thou hast heard of Robin Hood, — I am that outlaw, and these are my gallant followers.'

"' Unless report belie thee,' replied the knight, thou art a friend to the unfortunate. Dismiss me at once, and let me speed on/

"'Dine with us first,' said the forester, ' and freely shalt thou depart.' A cloth was spread beneath the shady branches, and covered with a profusion of the most delicious viands. Rhenish wine also, and ale plentifully abounded, and with cheerful hearts about twenty yeomen seated themselves around. ' Eat gladly, sir knight,' said Robin Hood; 'here's to thy health, and a more merry countenance ;' and as he spake he tossed off the contents of a goblet.

"' Thanks, thanks, my noble host,' replied the stranger; ' it grieves me that I shall ne'er be able to return thy goodness.'

"'Truly, good sir, thou look'st but grievous,' answered the outlaw. ' Tell me, is there aught in which my services can avail thee; what is the cause of thy deep sorrow^'

"' I have lost land and gold,' returned the knight, 'and I fear that my good name must follow them.' His tears burst out afresh. 'They call me,' he continued, ' Sir Rychard o' the Lee. I am sprung of

noble blood, and for these last three hundred years have mine ancestors wore spurs. r Twelve short months ago I had a noble house and fine estate, with four hundred pounds a year; but now, except my lovely wife and my sweet children, I have nothing in the world/

"' How hast thou lost thy riches *?' inquired Robin Hood anxiously.

"' Tis a short story,' replied the knight; '1 fought in a fair field with a knight of Lancashire, and slew him. To save my liberty, I mortgaged the broad lands of Wierysdale to St. Mary's Abbey, and if I pay not the amount to-morrow, my castle will be forfeited.'

"'What is the sum thou owest, and what wilt thou do if thou losest thy land*?' asked the outlaw.

"' Four hundred golden pounds must I pay, if I would keep fair Wierysdale,' he replied. 'I go to beg grace for another year; if the holy abbot will not grant it, I must flee away across the broad seas to a country where they know me not.'

"'Where are thy friends 4 ?' asked Little John; ' will they not be security for thee ?'

"' Alas,' replied Sir Ry chard, ' when I had money and house, and lands, I lacked not Mends, but now my oldest companions turn from me as a herd of deer would from a poor wounded hart. My only trust is in God and the blessed saints.'

"'Will Peter, or Paul, or John, be surety for thee *?' asked the outlaw. ' By my troth, good sir, thou must find wealthier friends than they/

"'I have none other,' replied the knight mournfully, 'except it be the Blessed Mary, who in all my trials has never failed me.'

"' Thou hast indeed a good friend,' said Robin Hood; ' and if thou wilt swear by our dear Lady that in twelve months from this day it shalt be restored to me, I will lend thee what thou wantest.' The knight fell upon his knees, gave the required promise, and drawing forth a silver image of the Virgin, he devoutly kissed it.

" ' In the meanwhile Little John had gone to the outlaws' treasury, and now returned with a heavy bag. He quickly counted out four hundred pieces of gold and offered them to the knight, with a beautiful doublet of scarlet cloth. These he readily

accepted. At Robin Hood's bidding, a gallant grey steed with rich housings was next brought forth, and after having received a pair of golden spurs from the hands of the noble outlaw, the knight vaulted into the saddle.

" ' 'Twould be a shame,' said Robin Hood, c that so well equipped a knight should ride without esquire; 'I will lend thee my brave man, Little John, until thou gettest a yeoman for thy service/ The forester willingly agreed, and mounting a stout palfrey, he was soon ready to accompany his new master. With tears of joy instead of sorrow, the knight bade farewell to his kind and generous host, struck his spurs into his new charger, and followed by Little John, galloped swiftly over the plain.

" On the morning after this adventure, the holy superior of St. Mary's Abbey, in the old city of York, was seated in his hall, attended by several of the monks.

"'Upon this day twelve months ago,' said he to his attentive listeners, ' there came a knight who borrowed four hundred pounds, upon the security of his lands and castle. The hour is near at hand; unless he appear and pay the money before yon glass has run, the fair lands of Wierysdale will belong to this sanctuary.'

" ' It is early yet, holy father, 5 replied the prior; ' the poor man may be in a far country, and it would be hard to use him thus harshly. Methinks thy conscience, my lord abbot, would but ill bear so rude a treatment to an • unfortunate knight.'

"'Thou art ever in my beard,' exclaimed the superior angrily. ' By all the saints I swear that, unless the knight of Wierysdale appear ere the sun has set, he shall be disinherited.'

"' He is either dead or he cannot pay,' said a fat monk, who was high cellarer, 'and St. Mary's Abbey will be enriched with a goodly sum. Shall I not seek the lord justice, holy father, and bid him attend to prepare deeds for the transfer of the land.'

"'Yea, brother,' replied the abbot; "tis but lost time to wait for our debtor, therefore use despatch, good brother—use despatch.' The cellarer left the room as quickly as his fat limbs would carry him, and in less than an hour returned with the lord chief justice.

" In the mean time Sir Ry chard o' the Lee and his esquire had arrived in York, and taken up their abode at an inn. After they had rested for awhile from the fatigue of their journey, they dressed themselves in their sorriest habiliments, and set out to the abbey. Upon knocking at the great gates, they were immediately admitted, and conducted into a lofty and spacious room, whose high pointed roof ornamented with grotesque images, narrow Gothic windows, and beautifully tesselated pavement, combined to strike the beholder with admiration, and increase his reverence for the inmates of such a noble dwelling.

"The knight and his attendant doffed their caps and bowed low as they entered the hall, and advanced to the upper end, where, upon a carved oaken throne, sat the abbot of St. Mary's, with the lord chief justice of York by his side.

" ' God save thee, holy father,' said the knight, as he kneeled before him; ' I have attended thee this day as thou didst bid me.'

" ' Hast thou brought any money, sir knight ^' asked the priest in a harsh tone.

"' Not one penny,' replied the suppliant. ' I am come to beg that thou wilt extend the time of payment for one more year.'

" ' That is unfortunate,' rejoined the abbot, with difficulty repressing his delight at the intelligence. ' The day is nearly gone, and unless thou canst pay down four hundred pounds ere the setting of the sun, thy lands must pass to the accruement of St. Mary's Abbey. Sir justice,' he continued, looking askance, ' here's to thee;' and in the height of his satisfaction he emptied a goblet of wine at a single draught.

" ' Good sir justice,' said the knight imploringly, 4 wilt thou not assist me in my distress. Day by day will I serve thee until I have repaid thy goodness.'

"'•Nay, sir,' returned the justice, 'I cannot do it if I had the will.' ' Give him two hundred pounds more, holy father, and the good knight will sign thee a release of the lands that he can no longer claim.'

" ' Never,' replied the knight fiercely, as he started to his feet. 'Merciless tyrants as ye are, ye get not my lands thus. Never shall monk or friar be heir to Wierysdale.

"' What,' cried the priest, rising from his seat; ' darest thou beard the abbot of St. Mary's; out

upon thee for a false knight, thy castle is no longer thine.'

"' ' Thou liest,' returned the knight, stamping his heel upon the pavement until it rung again: ' never was I false. I've stood in tournaments against noble earls and greater men than thou, and have oft proved myself a true knight and good. Take back thy gold,' he continued, as he poured out the contents of his purse at the abbot's feet; ' and think not that thou canst so easily get the fair lands of Wierysdale. Hadst thou shown courtesy to a suppliant knight, thou should'st have had recompense.' Then snatching away the papers which the justice had before him, Sir Rychard darted a look of defiance at the abbot, and with a firm step departed from the hall, leaving the holy father overwhelmed with astonishment, disappointment, and regret.

" Sir Rychard returned to his inn, gave away his old garments to the first beggar that passed by, and after dismissing his gallant esquire with the warmest thanks for his assistance, again started off with an attendant whom Little John had procured for him. He rode on, singing merrily, until he drew rein at

THE KNIGHT OF WIERYSDALE

his own gate in Wierysdale. His lady, with tears in her eyes, had been watching his approach, but when she saw the joyful countenance and proud bearing of her husband, she ran forth to clasp him in her arms, and learn the cause of such unexpected joy. The story was briefly told, and from that day to the end of their lives the good knight and his lady did not fail to remember in their prayers the name of Eobin Hood."

I had just finished this tale, when the chimes from the distant steeple faintly reached our ears. The hour at which we were expected back had arrived, and we were at least a quarter of an hour's walk away. We started to our feet, bounded through the wood, and over the low palings, and made many a passenger laugh heartily as we chased past him to our home.

OUR FIFTH MEETING.

REYNOLDE GRENELEFE.

THIS evening we resumed our old seats under the sycamore tree in the shrubbery, when I thus continued my tales: —

"After the departure of the knight of Wierysdale, Little John determined upon seeking an adventure, that he might have something to boast of among his companions, when he returned to Barnesdale woods. By chance he learned that there was to be a grand archery meeting near Nottingham, and that the high sheriff was to award a prize to the best marksman. Without delay, he rode across the country bypaths which no one but a daring forester would have chosen, and upon the next morning reached the appointed ground, just as the sports were about to commence.

" The best bowmen of the county had entered the lists, and as a silver bugle-horn was to be awarded to the victor, each man had resolved to do his best to gain it. Upon the appearance of the new competitor, they looked at each other, and after whispering together, laughed at the presumption of the stranger, who had dared to offer himself as their rival. One by one the well-known and oft victorious archers advanced, and shot their arrows so near the centre of the target that it was next to impossible to say whose aim had been the truest; Little John shot last, and with such success that his arrow knocked out one of the very nearest of his opponents'. The sheriff, surprised at his dexterity, rode up, examined the target and declared that he could not pronounce a decision. At the suggestion of the forester, to whom the others now paid greater respect, a thick white wand, which a ranger had been using to keep back the spectators, was placed upright in the ground at twenty paces farther distance. Again the sports began. — The Nottingham men supported their reputation, and no less than three arrows stuck in the mark; the outlaw fired last, and

I

also hit the wand. These four again shot, when two of the bowmen missed, and the contest remained to be decided between the first marksman of Nottingham, and the bold stranger.

" The populace had often given vent to their admiration of such gallant archery, by loud huzzas, but now a breathless silence prevailed. The sheriff, anxious for the honour of his county, rode up and down in a perfect fever of excitement, and spoke encouraging words to the Nottingham champion. The man coolly took up his position and drew his bow with the greatest care, but the shaft unfortunately flew half an inch above the mark. Little John smiled, advanced and shot his arrow a third time into the middle of the wand. A feeling of disappointment seemed to spread over the spectators, and the defeated archer could ill conceal his chagrin.

" 'Tell me, my good friend,' said the sheriff as he rode up to the victor, and presented him with the prize, ' what name bearest thou ? and what country dost thou dwell in *? '

"' My name is Reynolde Grenelefe,' replied the forester; ' I was born and bred in merry Holdernesse, and am now roving from town to town to seek a better fortune.'

"'By St. Hubert,' rejoined the sheriff, 'thou art the best archer that e'er drew bow in Nottingham. Wilt dwell with me, and protect the king's deer from the cursed outlaws *?'

"' Willingly, an thou'lt pay me well,' answered the forester boldly.

"' Thou shalt have forty pounds a year, and three new suits of clothes, and shalt dine every day off the king's venison,' said the sheriff.

"The artful forester readily agreed, and on the same day took up his abode in his new master's mansion, where he soon became on good terms with all the household, except the steward, who took a mortal aversion to him on account of his favour with their master. One day the sheriff went out hunting early in the morning, leaving Reynolde Grenelefe asleep in bed, where he lay until it was nearly noon; he then rose, and going to the kitchen, asked the steward for his dinner.

"' Thou lazy villain,' he replied, ' dost think thou hast earned it. By my troth thou shalt have neither to eat nor drink till my lord hears of thine idleness.'

" The forester laughed, and gave a stride towards the pantry door, but the steward was too quick for him : he turned the key in the lock, pulled it out, and placed it in his pocket. Without a word the outlaw stepped up and struck him with his open palm upon the ear, and the poor steward, stunned with the shock, fell heavily down. Reynolde then spurned the door with his foot, bursting lock and bar asunder, and entering the pantry, he found a goodly venison pasty and a bottle of strong ale, upon which, without either grace or ceremony, he began a most furious attack. While he was thus busy the cook came in, and seeing the steward lying on the floor, and the new servant devouring the contents of the pantry, he soon guessed the true state of the matter. Arming himself with a huge rolling pin, he crept quietly towards the offender, and before he could protect himself, struck him upon the back of his head; the outlaw well nigh fell, but catching at a board, he sustained himself, and then drawing his sw r ord, rushed at his cowardly

antagonist. For full an hour did they thump and belabour each other till they could scarcely stand. ' Give me thy hand,' cried Eeynolde, dropping his sword. ' Thou art a valiant fellow, and 'twere pity to break thy bones. Come with me to the woods ; I am one of Robin Hood's men, and if thou'lt join us we'll give thee a suit of Lincoln green, and teach thee the merry life of a forester.'

44 The cook consented; and after breaking open their master's treasury and seizing upon all the silver plate and money that it contained, the treacherous servants left the house, and mounting two of the finest horses in the sheriff's stable, galloped off with their booty to Barnesdale forest.

"Welcome, my brave yeoman. Where hast thou tarried? 1 exclaimed Robin Hood, as Little John presented himself and his companion before the gallant captain. 'And who bringest thou to the greenwood ?'

444 Thou shalt hear all, good master,' replied the tall forester. 'Thy worthy friend, the sheriff of Nottingham, hath sent thee his cook, his silver chalices, and three hundred golden pounds:' and he

related the story of his adventures with the greatest glee, while Robin Hood, who owed the poor sheriff many a grudge, laughed till the tears ran down his cheeks, and he was obliged to throw himself upon the grass from sheer exhaustion.

" Just as Little John was concluding his narration, a huntsman's bugle sounded in the distance. He stopped and listened for a moment. ' Tis my dear master's horn,' he exclaimed; ' I must away to him;' and darting through the woods, he ran over hill and dale until he reached the spot where the sheriff of Nottingham and his attendants were beating among the thickets in search of game.

" ' Ha! Reynolde Grenelefe,' he exclaimed, as his servant stood before him, ' where hast thou been ^'

"' Roving through the forest, good master,' replied Reynolde; ' and by my troth I have beheld the strangest sight that mortal eyes e'er saw. In yon dense wood is a fine stag, whose hide is of a bright green colour, and a herd of seven-score more lie scattered around him. His horns are so large and sharp that I dare not shoot for fear that he might rush at me and tear me, and hearing thy bugle-horn,

I have hastened to tell thee of so strange a creature.' The sheriff, filled with wonder, desired to be immediately conducted to the animal, and the outlaw started off again at his full speed, followed by his master until they arrived at the spot where Robin Hood was still lying upon the turf. 'This is the hart, good master,' said Little John, pointing to his captain; ' and there is the gallant herd; ' and he directed the sheriff's attention to a band of yeomen who were reclining under the shade of some neighbouring trees.

"'Thou hast betrayed me,' he cried, drawing his sword, and biting his lips with rage. 'Thus shalt thou suffer for thy treachery;' and he struck a fierce blow at his conductor.

"'Calm thee, good master,' exclaimed Little John, nimbly avoiding the weapon. 'Thou hast given me many a good dinner, and now thou shalt have a jovial supper in return.' Two foresters advanced, and gently disarmed the still threatening prisoner, who very quietly suffered himself to be seated at a well spread cloth. At the entreaty of the outlaws he began to eat; but when Little John brought him wine in his own cup, his mortification was so great that he could not swallow another morsel. The foresters pressed him so much the more, and laughed loud and long at his rueful countenance, while two or three sang ballads celebrating their own victory over the sheriff of Nottingham.

"The poor man could endure the scene no longer. He started to his feet, and would gladly have made his escape, but his flight was arrested. 'For one night, sir sheriff, thou shalt be an outlaw like us,' said Robin Hood to him. 'Thou shalt have thy couch under the green trees of Barnesdale, and if on the morrow thou likest thy fare, we will give thee a green mantle, and teach thee to shoot the grey goose-wing.' Night drew on; the foresters, wrapping themselves in their cloaks, laid themselves down under the most shady trees, and binding their prisoner, that he might not escape during the darkness, compelled him to share their broad couch. All night long he tossed about and groaned, and when, oppressed with weariness, he at length fell asleep, dreams of the most hideous nature wakened him to fresh torment. The darkness seemed to him interminable; but at length the sun rose, and the foresters one and all roused themselves from their slumbers. 'Hast thou passed a good night, sir sheriff?' asked Robin Hood. 'How likest thou our downy beds?'

" ' The beasts of the field lie more softly,' replied the sheriff. ' Eather than make me pass another night like this, I pray thee send an arrow through my heart, and I'll forgive thee. But wherefore dost thou detain me^ I have no gold, and that traitor Reynolde Grenelefe has robbed me of what I possessed at home. Suffer me to go and I will be thy best friend to my dying day.'

" c Swear that thou wilt never harm the foresters of Barnesdale,' replied Robin Hood, 'and thou shalt depart;' and he presented the cross of his sword to the sheriff's lips.

" He took the oath, and the outlaw immediately cut his bonds; then ordering his horse to be brought, he helped the anxious sheriff to his saddle, and bade him a merry ride. The goaded steed flew along the narrow pathway, and quickly emerging from the woods, bore his glad rider home to Nottingham.

THE MONKS OF ST. MARY S ABBEY.

"A twelvemonth was nearly elapsed since Robin Hood had lent the four hundred pounds to the knight of Wierysdale, and but two days yet remained to Lammas-tide, when the money would become due.

" By economy and service in arms the worthy knight had been enabled to save much more than the required sum. He purchased a hundred tough yew bows, with strings of twisted silk, a hundred beautiful quivers, well stored with arrows, each of which was notched with silver, feathered with the plume of a peacock, and tipped with a head of burnished gold ; and mounted on the outlaw's steed, he set out to Barnesdale wood, followed by a troop of his attendants, bearing the weapons of the chase before them.

"On his way the knight passed through a little town, where the inhabitants were celebrating a rural fair. The banks of a stream, over which he crossed by a rustic wooden bridge, were crowded with gaily dressed peasants, anxious to purchase the rare commodities which they were able only once a year to procure at this long-expected mart. There were tents of blue, and white, and crimson cloths, and long streaming banners floated proudly above them. There were open stalls too, and rich displays of costly goods, and the busy throngs, as they incessantly poured on and on, seemed full of merriment and gladness. It was a joyous scene, and the knight gazed upon it with heart-felt pleasure. He wished to join in it, but he remembered that the day was close at hand when he had promised re-payment to the generous outlaw, and he struck his spurs into his charger's sides. He had proceeded but a short way, when a loud noise broke upon the distant murmur that had hitherto reached him from the meadows, and caused him again to draw his rein. It seemed like the quarrelling of men in angry strife, and every moment it grew louder and louder. ' There may be need of our assistance,' said the knight to his followers ; and he instantly galloped to the spot whence the confusion arose. At the sight of a band of armed horsemen the crowd became calm, and opened a passage-way.

"' What means this uproar *? ' asked the leader. 4 Are ye not celebrating games of joy and peace'?' A dead silence prevailed. ' Tell me, my friend,' he continued, addressing one who stood nearest him, 4 why are ye thus at variance"? '

" ' Yon stranger,' replied the man, pointing to a gallant looking yeoman who rested upon his bow, apart from the rest; —' Yon stranger has borne off every prize this day. We know him not; and think 'tis unfair that the best men in our county should get no victory.'

"' Come hither, sirrah,' cried the knight to the offender. ' Who art thou that darest to shoot and wrestle better than any man in Nottinghamshire *?'

" The yeoman stepped forward boldly: —' What can it matter, sir knight, who I am ?' he replied. 6 I've won the prizes, and have a right to them, but these poor clowns cannot stomach a heavy fall, or my arrow in the centre of their bull's eye.'

" ' Shame on ye, my friends ; would ye wrong a victor of his lawful reward *?' exclaimed the knight, turning to the multitude. ; Where are the prizes *?' An old man advanced, and taking the horseman's bridle, led him to a tent, where were spread upon the grass a handsome saddle and bridle, ornamented with gold, the prize of the swiftest runner; a finely carved bow, and an arrow, three feet long, of the purest white silver, to be given to the truest marksman; and a pipe of the best Rhenish wine to be awarded to him who should gain the day at wrestling. All these had the stranger indubitably won; but when he demanded them, the disappointment of the native peasants broke out into loud mur-murings, and as few espoused the cause of the victor, it had well nigh gone hard with him. Staves had been brought into play, and more than one sword had been drawn, when the arrival of the knight and his attendants quieted the tumult

"' Hast thou a steed to bear this goodly saddle *?' said the knight to the stranger; ' and how wilt thou carry off this pipe of wine ^'

" ' I came a-foot,' replied the man ; ' but rather than leave so brave a prize, I will bear the saddle on my own back; as for the cask, these good peasants are welcome to it.'

"' Thou'rt a noble fellow,' returned the knight of Wierysdale, throwing him a purse of gold. 'There's for thy wine, and if thou wilt follow me, thou shalt have a charger for thy saddle.' The yeoman readily complied. One of the knight's men dismounted, and gave up his horse to him; he quickly clapped on his elegant furniture, and with the bow at his back, and quiver by his side, he sprung into the seat, and ranged himself with the rest of the attendants. The noble intercessor next ordered that the wine should be broached, and distributed to all who would partake of it. The command was quickly obeyed, amidst the cheers of the peasants, who soon forgot their previous quarrels and disappointments in the pleasures of the jovial cup. The knight waved his hand to them and rode on, but he had lost so much time at the fair, that the sun sank down long before he reached the woods of Barnesdale, and he was obliged to halt at a little cottage by the way-side.

" The morrow was Lammas-day; Robin Hood ordered a fat buck to be dressed, and preparations made for his expected guest; but noon passed without any appearance of him.

" ' Go thou/ said the outlaw to his favourite attendant, ' and see if thou canst espy this slothful knight. Take Will Scarlet and the Miller's Son with thee, and if his faithful surety send any over-bur-

dened travellers to pay my debt, bring them hither. But, I charge ye, if a poor man, or a merry jester, or a damsel in distress pass by, help them to your utmost, give them gold and assist them on their way.'

" The three foresters gladly obeyed, and soon reached the high road that ran through the wood. Many a stout yeoman and honest peasant did they encounter, and pass with a fair salutation, and one poor beggar, half clothed in rags, they sent on his path rejoicing. As they reached the summit of a hill, two monks riding upon palfreys, attended by about a score armed men on foot, and six sumpter mules heavily laden, appeared just ascending upon the opposite side.

"' I'll wager my best bow-string," exclaimed Little John, 'that these holy fathers have brought our captain's money. Bend your bows, my lads, and scatter the herd that follows them.' The foresters let fly arrow after arrow in such quick succession that the frightened travellers turned and fled precipitately ; the archers pursued, and soon gained upon the fugitives, who one and all rushed into the woods,

and endeavoured to escape amid the concealment of the foliage. Those on foot soon disappeared, but the two monks on their palfreys and the sumpter mules were easily captured by the outlaws. They immediately tied the hands of their prisoners behind them, and fastening the reins of their steeds together, they drove them to the presence of the chief, who doffed his cap, and advanced with great courtesy to meet his guests.

" I pray ye, holy fathers,' he said to them, ' take not offence at the rough usage of my followers. I care not to dine unless in goodly company, and therefore did they bring ye from your straight journeying.' The monks preserved a sullen silence, and suffered their bonds to be cut, and themselves dismounted without speaking a word.

"' Gramercy, good sirs,' cried Robin Hood, ' me-thinks ye have but a small share of courtesy. What holy house do ye inhabit ?'

" 'We are but poor brethren of St. Mary's Abbey,' replied one of the monks, who was the high cellarer, ' and were on our way to London to do reverence to the pope's legate, who has required our presence.'

"'May his blessing attend ye,' said the outlaw, in a mock solemn tone. ' Come now, my good friends, the feast is spread, sit ye and make merry.' It is probable that in their present condition the monks would have declined this request, had not the savoury odour that arose from a smoking haunch of venison and a roasted wild swan smoothed down their angry feelings. They were soon seated by the side of the gallant forester; sparkling wine was brought, and the health of the pope's legate was drunk with great glee. The monks ate heartily, and quaffed many a cup to their host and his merry men; forgetting, in their enjoyment, that they would pay dearly for the treat. Robin Hood laughed and sang, and his men trolled out their legendary ballads, till the sun had nearly reached the horizon.

"' I fear me,' said the outlaw to Little John, 'that our dear Lady is wroth with us. The day is well nigh spent, and our four hundred pounds are yet to come.'

"'Ne'er fear,' replied the tall forester. « These kind monks have brought it, I dare swear—for they come from her holy abbey. Tell us, good

K

fathers, have ye not repayment for us from your sainted patroness *?'

"' We have heard naught of this before,' replied the high cellarer. 'We possess but twenty marks wherewith to defray the expenses of our travelling. Let us away, kind sirs, or we shall ne'er reach Nottingham this night.'

"' If ye have but twenty marks,' returned Kobin Hood, 'ye will have to beg for charity ere ye reach your journey's end. See, my bold Little John, how much thou canst find in yonder heavy looking trunks. If 'tis as ye say I will charge ye nothing for your feast; but if ye have a prize, ye must e'en be content to part company with it.'

" Little John soon returned with the trunk upon his shoulders, and spreading his mantle upon the grass, he poured out a heap of gold upon it.

" ' Good master, here are eight hundred pounds or more,' he said, when he had counted out some few pieces and divided the rest into similar quantities. 'By my troth thou could'st not have wished for better payment.'

" The monks' vexation was now at its height; they bit their lips and cast anxious glances towards their palfreys.

"'Ye will need some few of these,' said, Robin Hood, as he gave a handful of golden pieces to each of them; 'the patron saint of St. Mary's has sent us the rest as repayment for the money we lent to the knight of Wierysdale.' They eagerly clutched the offered gold, and without opposition from the outlaws mounted their steeds with most surprising celerity, and, leaving the sumpter mules behind them, rode off amid loud shouts of laughter.

" The topmost branches of the trees alone were gilded with the rays of the setting sun, and the foliage had begun to cast a deeper shade, when a party of horsemen emerged from the woods upon the lawn where the bold foresters were merrily regaling themselves at the expense of the poor monks whom they had plundered.

" In an instant they started to their feet, and fifty shafts were levelled at the intruders, but when the foremost rider leaped from his horse and threw himself into the arms of Robin Hood, they easily recognised him as Sir Rychard o' the Lee. K 2

" ' Welcome, sir knight, thrice welcome/ exclaimed the outlaw. \ Truly thou look'st more merry than when last I saw thee in these woods ? Hast thou recovered thy fair domains *?'

"' Ten thousand thanks to thee, my noble, my generous friend/ cried the knight. ' I still hold my fathers' lands, and with the blessing of our Lady, I am come to return the sum I borrowed of thee.'

"' 'Tis already paid, my gallant sir,' returned Kobin Hood. 'Two monks from the Abbey of the Holy Virgin have this day brought me back my gold with interest; so keep thy money, and when thou seest a man in need, remember Eobin Hood.'

"'Nay, thou wilt overwhelm me with thy kindness,' replied the knight. ' I would have been with thee ere the noontide, but yonder knave had the audacity to win every prize at a village festival, and, had I not interceded, he would have received but a sorry recompense for his achievements.'

" ' Ha! hast thou one of my truest men among thy followers 2 ' exclaimed the outlaw, as he recognised the victor. ' George o' the Green would have stood toughly against a score of Jazy peasants, methinks.'

"'Yes, good master,' joined in the forester; 'but what can one arm do against three-score*? Of a truth I should have had a morning bath, an it had not been for this gallant knight.'

" Robin Hood whispered a few words to Little John, who left them and almost instantly returned with a bag of gold.

"' Take this, good sir,' said the chief outlaw, as he handed it to the knight. ' The monks of St. Mary's paid me too much by four hundred pounds. Thou canst not yet be rich; take it as a reward for thy generous intercession.'

" The knight would have refused, but he knew that by so doing he should displease his generous friend. ' I accept thy gift,' he replied. 'One day I may be able to repay thy goodness; till then I shall remain a heavy debtor. But I entreat thee, receive this poor present as a humble tribute of my gratitude ;' and at his command, his followers alighted from their steeds, and laid the bows and quivers at the outlaw's feet.

"The foresters all shouted for joy, as their chief distributed the handsome gifts among them. Many started off at once to try their new weapons; while the others resuming their seats upon the grass, helped the knight and his followers with unbounded liberality, and passed the rest of the evening in drinking and singing, till darkness closed upon their gaiety. Couches of fern and dried rushes were prepared for the guests, who slept soundly in the foresters' rude bowers, until the bugle-horn wakened them from their dreams, at the dawn of morning. The knight, anxious to return to his lady,stayed not to break his fast: bidding farewell to the kind outlaws, he sprung into his horse's saddle, and with his attendants rode off to his beloved home in Wierysdale."

OUR LAST EVENING.

THE GOLDEN ARROW.

MY legends of Kobin Hood were well nigh exhausted: the Midsummer holidays were drawing near, and we should soon be busily engaged in striving for the prizes that were awarded to the most proficient scholars.

"This is the last time I shall tell you of bold Kobin Hood," said I, when my school-fellows had gathered round me; "but if, after the holidays are passed, we all meet again, I will endeavour to find some other by-gone stories to relate to you, that I hope will be equally interesting." They thanked me warmly, and I thus continued: —

"When the monks of St. Mary's Abbey had escaped from the hands of the outlaws, they urged on their steeds to the utmost, nor did they draw rein until they reached the good town of Nottingham. Without delay, they sought the sheriff of the county, and made known to him the treatment they had received in the woods of Barnesdale.

" That worthy functionary listened with great attention to their complaint, and still burning with revenge for the many insults that he had received from the outlaws, he promised that he would rest neither night nor day till Robin Hood and his men were taken. Not knowing exactly how to accomplish this, to him, desirable object, he determined upon laying the matter before the king, and mounting his fleetest steed, he rode with great haste to London, where he demanded an audience of the valiant monarch, who had just returned from his long captivity in Austria.

" ' What!* cried Richard, when the sheriff had finished his complaint. ' Canst thou not take a sorry rebel who owns not a single castle *? Get thee gone for a coward. An thou dost not bring me that outlaw's head within half-a-year, thy shrievalty shall be given to a better man.'

" The poor sheriff felt his disgrace, and returned slowly home to Nottingham, pondering on the king's words, and devising plans by which he might retrieve his lost character. He thought of a notable scheme. He caused it to be proclaimed that an archery meeting would be held at Nottingham, and that a golden arrow would be given to the victor of the games. The day arrived, but he in vain looked for the coats of Lincoln green, that he had hoped would be among the crowd, and he rode about anxiously endeavouring to discover the outlaws of Sherwood. There were gallant yeomen in mantles of blue, and buff, and scarlet, and some there were in green, but they were good bowmen of Nottingham, and the sheriff was almost in despair. He ordered the sports to commence, and never was better archery shown before. A tall stranger, with a light blue jacket, excited the admiration of every one, and the arrow would have been his prize, but a rival yeoman followed and shot with such dexterity that he fairly eclipsed all those who had preceded him. He was dressed in a bright scarlet coat, crossed by a silken belt, from which was suspended a little bugle-horn of silver and gold; his lower limbs were clothed in the skin of a deer, bleached as white as snow; and upon his

head he wore a long black hood, which fell gracefully down his back.

" When the sports were concluded, this gay forester was unanimously declared the winner of the day, and amid the shouts of the spectators, he was led to the tent, beneath which the sheriff of Nottingham stood to award the golden arrow. The stranger fell upon one knee, and, with much praise of his gallant archery, the prize was delivered to him. He rose, placed the arrow in his belt, and a triumphant smile lighted up his features as, for one moment, he looked at the donor's face. It was enough, the sheriff caught the glance, and it acted like magic upon him.

"'Ho! guards, seize him!' he shouted with his utmost strength. c 'Tis Robin Hood, the outlawed rebel! Five hundred pounds for his head!' In a second, the forester had gained the middle of the field, and had blown a long shrill blast upon his horn. At the signal, yeomen flew from every part of the field and ranged themselves around him. The sheriff was astounded, he cried to his men to follow; and, mounting his horse, galloped towards the daring re-

THE GOLDEN ARROW.

bels. A flight of arrows met him half way, and his steed fell tumbling to the earth; the rider arose unhurt, but his men had fled on all sides, and he was obliged to follow them.

"' Base cowards,' he cried, ' ye shall be hung on the highest gibbets in Nottingham;' and snatching a huge crossbow from the hands of one of the fugitives, he levelled it at the retreating band and fired. One man dropped; it was the tall forester in the light blue coat.

" At this, the sheriff's followers took courage, and with a loud shout, dashed onwards in pursuit of the Outlaws, who had taken up their wounded companion, and were now full half a mile in advance. Arrows innumerable fell like hailstones on each party, and many of the Nottingham men fell, sorely hurt; but the chase continued, and the sheriff seemed still determined to pursue. For hours did the foresters use their fleetest speed, turning ever and again to discharge their bows, until they were well nigh exhausted. They would have stopped and fought, but the overwhelming numbers that pursued gave them but a poor chance of victory. In this extremity, a

young knight, riding upon a grey charger, and attended by several armed horsemen, met them upon the road. Surprised at so unusual a sight, the knight reined up his steed and disposed his men around him, as if to dispute the road. This bold step had well nigh proved his ruin. A hundred arrows were pointed at him, and, at a word, would have pierced through his breast-plate to his heart.

" ' Hold,' shouted Robin Hood, dropping his bow, 6 'tis Sir Rychard o' the Lee! Tis the good knight of Wierysdale. 5 The knight recognised the voice, leaped from his horse, and threw himself into the outlaw's arms. A few words briefly explained to him the reason of their flight.

" ' To my castle, to my castle/ he cried; ' 'tis close at hand, and will defy the sheriff of Nottingham, with ten thousand of his men.' Then vaulting into his saddle, he took the wounded forester, Little John? before him upon his steed, pointed out his fortress to Robin Hood and galloped away.

" The castle of Wierysdale, surrounded on every side by noble trees, stood upon a slight eminence in the middle of an extensive valley. The building itself was of immense strength; it was girded by a lofty stone wall, six feet in thickness, and two ditches of considerable breadth and depth encompassed it. Over these were bridges that could be raised or lowered at pleasure; and a strong iron door was the only way of entrance to the castle.

" The outlaws increased their speed, and soon reached this promised refuge. The gates were wide open ; they rushed in, and at a word the draw-bridges were raised, and the portcullis dropped. In a few more minutes the sheriff, with his followers at his heels, loudly demanded admittance. 'Sir knight,' he cried, ' if thou dost not deliver up the outlaws of Sherwood thou shalt be branded as a traitor.'

" ' Away, proud braggart,' retorted the knight. ' Dost thou threaten me *? By my good sword thou shalt one day rue thine insolence.' A. flight of arrows stopped farther parley, and the sheriff was in despair. It was useless, even with the multitude that he had at his command, to attempt forcing the castle, and the knight had set his authority at defiance. Burning

with disappointment and rage, he denounced him as a traitor to his king, and rushing through the mass who crowded behind him, he returned to Nottingham.

" For twelve days did Robin Hood and his foresters dwell with the good knight of Wierysdale, feasting upon the most delicate food, such as they seldom met with in their forest retreats. Little John's wound quickly healed, and ere long he winded his bugle-horn as merry as the rest, among the echoing woods of Barnesdale.

" The defeated sheriff neither forgot nor forgave the treatment that he had received. He was determined upon being revenged on the rebellious knight, and set spies round his castle to give him intelligence when he stirred from it. For a long time they watched in vain ; but one summer's morning the knight and his lady rode out to amuse themselves in the delightful sport of falconry. Their steeds bounded gaily along the meadows, by the banks of a river, and they rode far away from home. A solitary heron that had been patiently watching for fish in a shallow part of the stream, frightened at their approach, rose with a shrill scream, and soared high up in air. The lady checked her pal-

frey, untied the jesses that confined a falcon to her wrist, and threw it off. The bird flew upwards as if shot from a bow, and rapidly ascended higher than the quarry: fluttering its wing, it hovered for an instant above, and then shooting downwards, struck the heron with its sharp beak and bore it to the earth. The lady was delighted, and applying a silver whistle to her mouth, recalled the well-trained hawk, which flew back again to her hand, and seemed proud of her caresses. Pleased with the sport, they galloped over many a verdant plain and flowery mead, and noon was long past ere they bethought themselves of returning. They were conversing about Robin Hood and his bold foresters, and wondering that they had heard nothing more of the sheriff of Nottingham, when they became aware of six armed horsemen galloping towards them at their utmost speed. Little imagining their intentions, the knight quietly pursued his course, when, to his surprise, the men checked their steeds as they approached, and with drawn swords in their hands surrounded him. In the leader the unfortunate knight easily recognised the sheriff of Nottingham, and he guessed his fate. He was fastened with thongs to his

saddle, his arms were tied behind his back, and he was led away captive.

" His lady, aware that resistance was fruitless, turned her horse's head, and galloped swiftly from the spot. Full of courage and love for her gallant husband, she rode on without drawing rein until she reached the forest of Sherwood, into which she fearlessly entered. A youth was lying upon the grass under a broad tree. ' My friend,' she cried to him, ' canst tell me where to find bold Robin Hood ?'

" The young man started to his feet, and doffing his cap, replied, ' I am one of Robin Hood's foresters, gracious lady, and will conduct thee to him; ' and taking the palfrey's rein in his hand, he led it through the narrow paths to the spot where the bold outlaw was shading himself from the summer's heat beneath a rustic bower.

" ' God save thee, good Robin Hood,' said the lady as the forester advanced; ' grant me thine aid, and that quickly. Thine enemy, the sheriff, hath bound my dear husband, and led him captive to Nottingham/

" The outlaw replied by setting his bugle-horn to

his lips, and sounding a shrill blast, it was answered from every side, and seven-score men soon gathered round him.

"' Busk ye, my merry men,' he cried to them. ' To the rescue of the knight of Wierysdale. That double villain, the sheriff of Nottingham, hath bound him. He that will not fight for our good friend is no longer follower of mine/

" The men gave a loud shout to prove their readiness, and their captain, bidding the lady be of good cheer, and await the issue in her castle, darted through the woods. The foresters followed him in a crowd close upon his heels; neither hedge nor stream stopped their progress; they leaped over every obstacle, and in two hours reached the town of Nottingham. They were just in time. The gaoler was even at the moment unbarring the gates of the castle to admit the prisoner, and the sheriff was unfastening the bonds by which he was held to his horse. At the appearance of the outlaws a loud cry was raised by the astonished inha. bitants, and the sheriff leaped into his saddle. He had but a small force at hand, quite insufficient to oppose the assailants, and seizing his prisoner's bridle

L

rein, he attempted to fly ; — 'twas too late. An arrow from the bow of the foremost outlaw pierced his brain, and he fell headlong from his steed. His attendants were routed, and the knight of Wierysdale was recaptured. Robin Hood himself cut his bonds with a dagger, and after raising a loud shout of victory, he and his gallant foresters retired to Wierysdale, where they received the warm thanks of the lady of the castle, and after partaking of a glorious feast, they returned to their wonted abodes in merry Sherwood.

ROBIN HOOD'S PARDON, REBELLION, AND DEATH.

" The excitement caused by the death of the sheriff of Nottingham was not easily appeased. Intelligence of the outrage was carried to King Richard, who summoned a council to devise the best means of putting down the fearless rebels. They declared the knight of Wierysdale an outlaw; and his lands, which were forfeited to the crown, were offered as a reward to whomsoever should take the traitor, Robin Hood, dead or alive. Fifty knights volunteered their services, and Sherwood forest became too hot for the brave outlaws, who retired by stealth to Plompton park, in Cumberland, where they concealed themselves for many weeks. At last, receiving intelligence that the search was abandoned, they ventured to return to Sherwood; but, to their great surprise, they were one morning interrupted by the approach of six priests, who advanced towards them, riding upon steeds richly caparisoned. The foremost was a man of most commanding presence. He was of noble countenance, tall stature, well proportioned, and apparently of Herculean strength; and, as he sat upright upon his saddle and glanced around him, his stately mien but ill accorded with the peaceful character of the white robe that covered him.

" Robin Hood knew him not, and wondered what bold bishop it could be, who had ventured to enter upon the proscribed domains.

" ' By thy leave, holy father,' he cried, as he stepped from a thicket, and laid his hand upon the horse's bridle, ' thou must abide awhile. If thou hast gold in thy purse, by the laws of Sherwood forest it is forfeited.'

" ' Good sir,' replied the bishop, ' I have but L 2 forty pounds. King Richard has been at Nottingham, and the gay follies of the court have swallowed up the rest;' and drawing a purse from his girdle, he gave it to the outlaw, who counted out the bright gold pieces into his hand. 'Thou wilt need these, perchance,' he said, as he gave back half the money. ' We may meet again and thou canst then repay me.'

" ' Gramercy, but thou art a gentle thief,' exclaimed the bishop. ' If, as I strongly suspect, thou art bold Robin Hood, Richard, king of England, sends thee his seal by me, and bids thee attend him in the good town of Nottingham.'

" The outlaw bent his knee as he beheld the royal signet. ' I will obey,' he cried, ' I can trust to the honour of King Richard, and for love of him, sir bishop, thou shalt dine with me under our try sting tree. He winded his bugle-horn merrily, and seven-score men obeyed the summons.

" A cloth was spread upon the grass, and plentifully supplied with venison, fowls, and fish; cans of fine brown ale, and bowls of ruby wine. The bishop and his companions seated themselves, and a jovial feast ensued. c Let us drink to the health of
King Richard,' cried the outlaw, filling his goblet to the brim. ' He who fails me in this pledge is no friend of Robin Hood's.' Loud cries of ' Long live the King,' rose from all sides; and in imitation of their host, each man emptied his cup, and reversed it upon the cloth before him.

" ' Bend your bows, my gallant followers,' said the outlaw, ' and show our guests the archery of Sherwood.' A willow wand was fixed in the earth, at a long distance off, and a garland of wild roses was suspended upon its top. The laws of the game were, that whoever missed the garland should lose his bow and arrows, and receive a buffet upon his bare head. One by one the foresters advanced, and all shot true, until Little John carelessly missed the wand by three good inches. Robin Hood gave him a blow upon his ear that made it ring for many an after hour, and then took his own turn. To his great dismay his shaft flew on the outer side of the garland.

" His men shouted with laughter. ' Thou hast lost thy bow, good master!' they cried in the greatest glee. ' The bishop shall give thee thy pay.' The priest
laughed too, and turning up the sleeves of his gown stepped toward the outlaw.

" Robin Hood stood firm, and folded his arms upon his breast, but the stalwart bishop bestowed such a buffet upon his head that he rolled over and over upon the grass.

"' By my troth,' cried he, when he had recovered his feet, there is pith in that arm of thine. I'll warrant me thou canst shoot a bow as well as us. The bishop laughed again, and taking up Robin Hood's forfeited weapon, let fly at the garland. The arrow, too strongly shot, flew above the wand, and struck into a tree on the further side of the lawn.

"'Now thou must take thy pay,' exclaimed the outlaw; and striding towards him, he gave him a vigorous blow, but the priest did not waver an inch. At that instant a horseman galloped swiftly across the plain, and leaping from his steed, ran to them : it was the knight of Wierysdale. ' Away, my brave men, — away,' he shouted; ' King Richard is seeking for ye. The forest is beset with men, and ye will '

He suddenly paused; his eye had caught the keen glance with which the bishop was regarding him. He

THE OUTLAWS ALLEGIANCE

threw himself at his feet: — ' Pardon, gracious sire,' he exclaimed, ' one who has served thee long and faithfully.' Kobin Hood was struck dumb — the truth flashed across his mind : — it was King Richard whom he had so unceremoniously buffeted. He fell upon his knees by the knight's side, and sued for mercy.

4< ' Sir knight,' exclaimed the noble king, ' thou hast done wrong, but I forgive thee ; rise, — thy lands are restored to thee. As for thee, thou valiant traitor, he continued, placing his hand on Robin Hood's head, ' on one condition only can I grant thy pardon. Thou and thy men must follow me to London, and be my royal archers.' The outlaws shouted with rapture; cries of ' Long live King Richard' rent the air, and every man bent his knee to their royal master.

" The king then mounted his palfrey and retired, accompanied by Robin Hood, Little John, and Will Scarlet, each of whom he soon afterwards appointed to some place of dignity. Many of the foresters dispersed to various parts, but fifty of the most faithful followed their beloved master to London.

" Here, it is said, our brave hero assumed his title of earl of Huntingdon, and lived in most noble style ;

but soon growing tired of the confinement of the court, he asked permission to revisit the merry woods. The king granted him seven days, but when Robin Hood breathed the delightful air of Sherwood, and heard the songs of the sweet birds, he could not tear himself away. He ranged through many a well-known thicket and oft-frequented lawn, and in the ecstacy of his delight he set his bugle horn to his mouth, and made the old trees re-echo with the blast. To his great astonishment it was replied to, and four-score youths bounded towards him. Several had deserted him in London, and many who were at first disbanded had returned to their favourite haunts, and Robin Hood was again acknowledged as the leader of a forest band. Little John and Will Scarlet soon learned the intelligence, and with all speed joined him with the rest.

" King Richard was enraged; he sent a renowned knight with two hundred soldiers to capture the rebellious outlaw, and a desperate fight took place upon a plain in Sherwood forest. It lasted from sunrise to sun-set, but neither party could boast of victory, and the knight lost many of his men. Robin Hood himself was wounded by an arrow, and was obliged to be taken to Kirkleys Nunnery, where he was treacherously suffered to bleed to death by the prioress. As he found his end approaching he called Little John to him. ' Carry me into the woods, I entreat thee,' he said to him;

"'And give me my bent bow in my hand, And a broad arrow I'll let flee; And where this arrow is taken up There shall my grave digged be."

"The outlaw shot his last bow. His shaft flew feebly to a short distance, and fell beneath an oak. He leaned back into the arms of his faithful attendant — and died. His wish was complied with ; and a stone was placed upon the green sod to mark the last resting-place of the brave Robin Hood ; it bore this inscription: —

I was obliged to hurry the latter part of my stories more than I could have wished, but I had scarcely finished, before our faithful monitor, the sonorous school bell, called us to our less pleasing, but more important pursuits.

The holidays soon after commenced, and we all returned HOME.

THE END.

Made in the USA
Columbia, SC
27 February 2022